PLAY THE GAME

BY JOEL CROWSON

© 2022

Richard Albert Crowson and T. Neal Crowson

This book is dedicated to my great-uncle, Thomas Neal Crowson (Krau-son), whose unique life experiences and personal journal were the catalysts for this story.

In Memoriam

To Mildred Walker, a dear friend, family counselor, and the adopted grandmother of my three daughters. Thank you for your kindness, encouragement, and sound advice. And thank you for being adamant that I send this manuscript to Trilogy Publishing. We will miss you.

Acknowledgments

First, I want to thank my three daughters, Joanna, Whitney, and Meredith, who lend color and excitement to every day, and to my wife, Anna Beth, for being my cheerleader during the good times and my encourager through the tough times, for putting up with my moody days and restless nights, and for believing in me oftentimes more than I believed in myself. I can never thank you enough.

Leslie L. Crowson, Sr., my dad, for sharing Uncle Neal's story and gifting his journal to me.

Blanche Lockhart Crowson, my mom, for her encouragement, humor, and sharp eye when reading the rough draft of this book.

First United Methodist Church of Shreveport, for occasionally providing a quiet space for me to write.

Thomas and Linda Richardson, for allowing me to use a variation of Linda's nickname, Suby, for one of my characters, and for providing a quiet, secluded place on their farm for me to write.

Rusty Poland, for information on Bienville Parish cemeteries and for directing to the two-volume set entitled *History of Bienville Parish*, written by his mother, Billie Gene Poland.

Demetrio Botello, Jr., for editing the Spanish dialogue.

My siblings, who gave me much encouragement through the years—Carol Crowson DeVille, Leslie L. Crowson, Jr., R. Lyndon Crowson, Kathy Crowson Leaphart, Cyndi Crowson Nunn, and Donna Crowson Lewis.

Table of Contents

Chapter 1: The Navy

The crowd noise was deafening! The tension and excitement were suffocating! The Bienville Bobcats were down 1–0 with two outs in the bottom of the ninth. Ruston just needed one out to win the game. Bienville had runners on first and second with a good hitter at the plate, but he'd been in a slump through the playoffs. He was a sure pull hitter to left field, and everyone knew it. Ruston's outfield was positioned tight to the left, leaving right field wide open.

The runner on first base was Neal Crowson, a threat at any position on the field. There was bad blood between Neal and Ernie Colvin, Ruston's pitcher, and the Ruston coach knew it. He yelled out to the mound, "Focus on the batter! Forget the runners! Just focus on the batter!"

The first pitch was a heater down the pipe for strike one. Ruston's fans cheered in anticipation of the win. Striding back to the mound, Ernie checked the runners. Pete stayed close at second; Neal was two steps off at first. Earnie glared at him for a second, then turned and fired an off-speed pitch across the plate. It was a swing and a miss for strike two. The batter at the plate was scared silly, and Ernie could smell the fear.

Neal stood at first base. The sweat ran down his face in the sweltering Louisiana summer heat. He knew it was time to take risks. He also knew that Ernie hated his guts, and maybe he could use that to his advantage.

He took a lead off first base; it was a classic balance of wits between pitcher, batter, and runners. Ernie feigned a pick-off at first, then spun toward second; Pete returned to the bag. Ernie turned around and resumed his place on the mound, focusing on the batter.

"Pete!" Neal yelled. "Watch for a ball but run on the swing!" Pete nodded. Neal took a risky lead. Again, Ernie turned and faked a throw. Neal leaned toward first, then stood his ground. Ernie glared at him. Neal smiled back and took one step back toward first.

"Forget the runners! Get the out!" the Ruston coach screamed.

Ernie took his position back on the mound. Neal took a dangerous lead off first. Ernie glanced over and locked eyes with Neal. His eyes seethed with animosity, but his jeering smirk bore an air of impending victory. Neal took another step away from first, taunting him, daring him to try a pick-off. Again, Ruston's coach screamed, "Forget the runners!" Ernie turned back to the plate, then made one last glance at the runners. He knew he should focus on the lead runner, but his bad blood with Neal ran too deep for him to ignore. One last time he cast an eye at Neal, who was way off the base. The temptation was strong but controllable; until Neal smiled and blew him a kiss.

Furious, Ernie lost it. He spun around for the pick-off, and with all his strength, threw the ball directly at Neal...and way down the right-field line. Neal took off, yelling at Pete, "Go! Go! Go!" He rounded second base and, in what seemed like an instant, was rounding third. Without hesitation, he was on his way home. Pete crossed home plate to tie the score. The right fielder finally got to the ball, scooped it up, and let it fly. The fans went crazy; the noise was deafening. But all Neal saw was home plate, and all he heard was instinct telling him to run.

The throw from right field was coming like a bullet. Neal was flying down the line. They were on a collision course at home plate. The catcher stepped inside the baseline to catch the underthrown ball. Neal dove headfirst, body outside the line, and hand stretched out as far as he could reach. The catcher's swipe at Neal was high, and Neal's hand slid under the glove and across the plate. "Safe!" the umpire yelled, slinging his hands out to his sides. "He's safe!"

The Bienville Bobcats went crazy! The fans screamed with joy, jumping and screaming and running onto the field as if they'd won the National Championship. The speechless Ruston fans watched in disbelief. The small town of Bienville had defeated the much larger Ruston by a score of two to one. The underdogs had won the league championship!

Soon the celebration died down, and Neal was collecting his gear when a gentleman he didn't recognize approached him. "Nice game, Mr. Crowson."

"Thanks," Neal responds.

"My name is Veldon Maxwell. Can we talk for a moment? I have an interesting proposition for you."

Neal turned to Mr. Maxwell. "A proposition?"

"Yes."

Neal hesitated for a moment. "Okay. Let's get out of the sun. I've had enough heat for one day."

As they made their way to the shade of an old live oak tree, one of Neal's teammates walked by. "Nice game, Mr. Baseball!" Neal grinned and nodded in response.

Mr. Maxwell smiled, "Mr. Baseball?"

"Yeah. They joke a lot."

Neal sat cross-legged on the ground. Mr. Maxwell took a seat near him on a log. "Neal, I'm a scout for the Shreveport Pirates baseball team, Texas League. Mr. Busby, our manager, asked me to check you out, which I have for several games now. You know, you've created quite a stir in the league."

"Really?"

"Yes, quite a stir! You're a top prospect for practically every team in the country. And the National League, I should say."

Neal sat motionless in thought. This was his dream. From an early age, playing in the big leagues was his dream. But even in his wildest dreams, he never thought it could be true. He was a small-town boy from a surveyor's family. He had always thought surveying, or farming, maybe, would be his life. But now, in an instant, his dream had become plausible. The Texas League. The National League, even. That was his dream.

But it wasn't his plan. He'd always seen dreams as just that, and he'd been taught that a man must have a plan. And he had his. "Mr. Maxwell, I must say, you've given me a reason for pause."

"Pause? Son, what I've given you is a chance of a lifetime! Men who pause, well, they often get left behind."

Neal nodded. "I know, sir, but the timing…. I've made plans."

"Plans? What plans could offer you more than professional baseball?" Neal sat for a moment, trying to arrange his thoughts. Mr. Maxwell continued, "You'd be doing what you love. Baseball! You'd get to travel around the country, meet people you've only heard of, see cities you've only read about in books! What could be better than that?"

Neal turned to him and said, "Travelling around the *world*, meeting people I've *never* heard of, and seeing *countries* that I've only read about in books."

Mr. Maxwell stared at him wide-eyed. Neal sensed his confusion.

"You see, Mr. Maxwell, I leave next week to join the Navy. I'm signing up for the president's Great White Fleet. Have you heard?"

"Ah, yes. President Roosevelt's Great White Fleet. The whole nation has heard. I've read much about it in the papers; potentially a very interesting cruise." He paused, "But no guarantee you'll get the assignment."

"Yes, that's true."

"All the more reason to sign with me and the Pirates, young man."

"I do admit, Mr. Maxwell, it is very intriguing…and tempting! But I have to do this. I *have* to, you know?"

Mr. Maxwell smiled and nodded his head. "Neal, I respect any young man who puts duty and patriotism ahead of his dreams. Who knows, if I was a young man like you, I might just go with you and sign up myself! But are you sure?"

"Ha! Yes, I'm sure. Besides, I'm young. Maybe when I get back, I'll look you up."

"Maybe so. But things change, you know. People change; times change. The league is changing, expanding so fast it may be totally different when you get back. There's no guarantee of a second chance, you know. But you look me up. You *do* look me up when you get back."

Neal hopped up, grabbed his bat and glove, and turned to the scout. "I'm honored, Mr. Veldon Maxwell, scout for the Shreveport Pirates! Thank you."

"My pleasure."

Veldon watched as Neal walked away. "Don't forget me!" Neal shouted.

Maxwell waved a hand and mumbled to himself, "Not likely, Mr. Baseball. Not likely!"

Chapter 2: Enlistment

Neal enlisted on Tuesday, July 29, 1907, and within a few days, he arrived at Hampton Roads, the main port in Norfolk, Virginia. There he was relieved of his hair and outfitted with the latest in navy apparel. He began his training in earnest and was soon recognized as a man who was disciplined, educated, and wise beyond his years.

He was selected for the rank of petty officer of the Ninth Company by Instructor Durgin, and a few days later, his appointment was announced to the entire battalion by Commander in Chief H. Moore.

The Jamestown Tercentennial Exposition served as the 1907 World's Fair. It had started on April 26th and was scheduled to end on November 30th. It was being held on a 130-acre plot just up the hill from the main docking area at Hampton Roads. This celebration of the 300th anniversary of the settling of Jamestown was the biggest celebration Neal had ever seen.

There was every kind of exhibit one could imagine, and every day offered a selection of festivities to suit any interest. Duties aboard the ships were continuous and challenging, but plenty of time was allowed onshore for the men to visit the exposition.

One of the many celebrations scheduled at the exposition included a military parade. Neal was excited to learn that the Ninth Company was to march in the parade. He and the rest of the men were filled with anticipation. They would finally be able to use the marching skills they had sweated to learn. With a little practice, they would fine-tune their skills, synchronize their steps, and move as if they were a single body. They looked forward to the challenge; the Ninth Company would be second to no one.

Hard work and rigorous athletics had sculpted Neal into a powerful, muscular man. He was a striking figure in his dress uniform, and he was blessed with the good looks to go with it. He was told that he didn't have to march in the parade; as a petty officer, he was privileged to ride on a float. He was a bit apprehensive about it, but his peers encouraged him to ride. He was also welcome at the debutante ball, but only as a spectator. The guests at the banquet table were there by invitation only.

The parade had all the entries one would expect. A couple of marching bands, rolling exhibits called "floats" that were decorated to the hilt, and street performers marching in and out of the procession, stopping now and then to perform their magic and draw applause from the crowds of onlookers. It also had floats celebrating Robert Fulton and his steam engine, the most esteemed invention of the day. There were several floats extolling the Great White Fleet, the last in line being the one upon which Neal was to be riding. Behind his float was a fine motorcar. A driver opened the door to allow entry of what must have been an affluent and important couple. And standing beside the car was the most beautiful young woman Neal had ever seen.

Neal was captivated. He had never witnessed a woman so striking. It wasn't because she was obviously wealthy; there were many wealthy families in Louisiana and no shortage of beautiful ladies. But she was...different. Her clothes were immaculate, with attention given to every detail and fitted to accentuate every curve. Her demeanor reflected great training and probably years at an Eastern finishing school. Her face was angelic, appearing without flaw.

But there was something more than that, something Neal couldn't put his finger on. Something invisible that resonated deep in his soul. Suddenly, Neal's eyes met hers, and, for a moment, they both remained transfixed. Then she coyly turned away and got into the car.

He continued to stare for a moment, but his attention was intercepted when he was summoned by one of the parade coordinators. Following the coordinator's directions, he climbed onto the floating deck and positioned himself by the side rail. When everyone was in place, the float coordinator instructed them to engage the crowd as much as possible and enjoy the ride.

Soon the parade began to move, and the long line of entries began to proceed down the street. His comrades on the float waved and cheered and shouted pleasantries at the throng of onlookers. Neal did his best to engage, but try as he may, he couldn't erase the vision of the woman who had looked into his eyes and infatuated his soul. Frequently, he looked back at the car, trying to get a glimpse of this exquisite woman but rarely having any success. He had to see her again; he knew that. He must talk to her, learn all he could about her thoughts, her needs, her wants, her desires...her life.

Chapter 3: Robert Fulton Day

The Robert Fulton Day ball was amazing! The dining hall at the New York State Building was packed wall to wall with exposition attendees, politicians, and many citizens of extreme wealth and status. Men wore suits and ties and flashy shoes and gold pocket watches. Ladies paraded around in long flowing gowns, tight waisted, decorated with all types of lace, satins, silks, and flowers. Necklines ranged from high collared to low cut. Most wore hats, and expensive jewelry was on display everywhere. Neal had never seen this level of extravagance.

From his vantage point at the entry of the dining hall, he could see nothing but a mass of humanity mingling like ants in a disturbed anthill. He stood against the wall for a while, admiring the decorations, the architecture, the people, and the richness of the setting, the likes of which he had never seen. As he scanned the huge dining room, he soon spied an *hors d'oeuvre* table at the rear of the hall.

A straight path to the table was impossible. He threaded his way through the crowd by following the paths of least resistance. As he neared the west side of the room, he saw her. She was only a few steps away and appeared to be unaccompanied. Before Neal could move, a large, well-dressed man stepped up to her, grabbed her around the waist, and pulled her close. She threw her hands into his chest and pushed him away. He grabbed her by the arm and again pulled her to his chest, then wrapped his left arm around the small of her back. Neal pushed his way through the crowd and seized the man's wrist, firmly twisting it hard enough to force him to release his hold on her.

"It appears, sir," Neal said, "the woman has no interest in your topic of discussion."

"Who do you think you are?"

Neal increased his grip. "It isn't about me, sir."

"Butt out, or I will ruin you!"

Neal dug his strong fingers into the man's wrist. "Possibly. But unless you release the lady, you won't be physically able for quite some time." The brute released her, and she darted behind Neal and clutched his arm. Neal released his wrist. The man straightened his jacket. "It's a good thing you're in uniform!"

"Yes, it is," Neal said. Several witnesses to the scuffle clapped and cheered as Neal watched the degenerate turn and disappear into the crowd. He then turned to this beautiful woman who was still holding his arm and smiled. "He's done."

She laughed. "Yes, I believe his goose is cooked!" They laughed for a moment, then Neal asked, "May we talk?"

"Absolutely." She extended her gloved hand to Neal. He took it in his and gazed into her eyes.

She leaned in close. "There's a veranda just outside. It'll be a bit quieter there. Of course, there will still be plenty of eyes to keep you honest. You know, just in case you're a scoundrel too!"

"I could be," Neal laughed.

"You could, but somehow I think not."

They made their way through the crowd and stepped out into a mild, late September evening.

"This is nice," she said.

"Um-hm," Neal replied. "Do you realize, ma'am, I don't even know your name?"

"Well, I declare, sir," she teased. "You surely don't."

Neal waited, but she said nothing. "Okay," he laughed. "My name is Neal Crowson, Petty Officer Neal Crowson."

"Nice to meet you, Officer Crowson." She extended her hand and said, "I'm Katherine Bailey, Miss Katherine Bailey."

Neal took her hand in his and gave it a modest shake. "Nice to meet you, Miss Bailey."

She laughed. "For goodness' sake, just call me Katherine. May I call you Neal?"

"Please do," he laughed.

The light banter that followed flowed naturally, not strained or awkward. Neal spent just a short time on the small talk, then plunged into the more intimate details. He asked her where she was from and about her family. He was impressed that her father was a U. S. senator, Joseph Bailey. He asked about her home, her hobbies, what she did for fun. He especially liked her love for baseball. She talked of attending the games at West End Park to watch the Houston Buffalos. Neal told her of his love for baseball and the chance he had to play for the Shreveport Pirates. She was impressed by his decision to serve his country but told him she hoped to see him play one day. She also told him that she remembers seeing him at the parade. Neal was surprised but pleased.

The crowd in and around the New York State Building was called to attention. Mr. Poland Littleton, the event moderator, announced that it was time for those guests attending the dinner to make their way to the banquet hall.

Katherine grabbed Neal's hands. "Neal, come with me to the dinner. Be my guest."

"I'm not on the list, Katherine. I'm sure there's no room."

"Nonsense! I'll talk to Father. He'll arrange it."

"He doesn't know me…. I'm just—"

"You're my guest. Besides, how could Father refuse the man who defended my honor?"

Katherine led Neal to the banquet hall, and it took just a few moments for her to find her father. The senator spotted them as they approached. His interest was piqued to see his daughter leading a handsome young man by the hand.

"Well, how refreshing!" Looking at Neal, he added, "She usually shuns brazen young suitors, as well as old ones, for that matter."

Neal grinned.

"Father, please!" Katherine responded. "He's neither brazen nor a suitor."

"Well, what might he be then?"

"Just the man who defended your daughter's honor. Rescued me from the clutches of a scoundrel, he did."

"I should say! And what might this chivalrous young man's name be?"

"His name is Neal Crowson, Petty Officer Neal Crowson, recently assigned to the U. S. S. Minnesota of the president's Great White Fleet."

"Well, Mr. Petty Officer Neal Crowson, it's good to make your acquaintance." He extended his hand to Neal. "I'm her father, Joseph Bailey."

Neal gripped his hand and nodded. "It's good to meet you, sir."

"And my sincerest thanks for rescuing Katherine from what must have been a life-threatening situation, I'm sure."

"Oh, Father! You're impertinent! Besides, the fiend had me in his clutches, and Neal forced him to release me. I'm very thankful!"

"As am I, my dear. Sincerely, thank you, Neal."

"My pleasure."

"Father, I think it only proper to invite Neal to dine with us. In fact, I already have. Please, Father, can't we find him a chair?"

"I'm sure of it! This dinner is set in honor of all kinds of heroes," Senator Bailey teased. "Actually," the senator turned to Neal, "Mrs. Bailey just left with a headache, which leaves her seat open. Please join us."

"I would be honored, sir. Thank you."

Senator Bailey led them across the banquet hall. He whispered something to the headwaiter, who promptly led them to three open seats at one of the tables.

"Impressive," Neal whispered to Katherine.

"Position has its privileges, so they say," she smiled. "But you should know something about that, considering your father's position."

"Some privileges, maybe, but not to this degree," Neal responded. "Besides, my father is just a civil engineer, not an oil tycoon."

"Yes, but he's done well, not to speak of his impressive position with the Freemasonry organization. We know those mysterious men are usually quite at home in luxurious surroundings."

"That's true, but this...this is magnificent!"

As the tables filled up and the crowd settled in, a stately couple approached and greeted Katherine and Senator Bailey. The senator addressed them both by name and was very warm and inviting, but Neal could tell Katherine remained a bit distant.

The man smiled at Katherine. "Beautiful as ever, Katherine."

"How are you, Dr. George, Mrs. Akers?"

"We're well," Dr. Akers replied. "And may I ask, who is this young gentleman?"

"Dr. George, this is Petty Officer Neal Crowson. Neal, this

is Dr. and Mrs. George Akers."

Neal nodded at the couple. "Nice to meet you, Dr. and Mrs. Akers."

"Likewise, Neal. Any friend of Katherine's is a friend of mine. Have you two been acquainted long?"

"Well, as a matter of fact, we—"

Neal's answer was interrupted when, once again, Poland Littleton welcomes everyone and tells them to be seated and enjoy their meal during the program. Dr. and Mrs. Akers took seats on the opposite side of Katherine, with Dr. Akers sitting uncomfortably close at her side. Katherine looked at Neal and, with a scowl, indicated her dislike of the man.

Neal smiled and, to ease the tension, he engaged her in light conversation.

Several speakers addressed the crowd, including Retired Rear Admiral Purnell Harrington, USN; Governor Hughes of New York; Governor Swanson of Virginia; Ex-President Grover Cleveland; Samuel Clemens (Mark Twain); Fulton's grandson Robert Fulton Ludlow; and Mrs. Donald McLean, President-General of the Daughters of the Fathers of the Republic. Attendees included dignitaries from all over the U. S. and around the world.

Neal relished the extravagance and fanfare of the event. But his focus was still Katherine. She was mesmerizing, radiant in her appearance, perfect in etiquette, and physically exquisite. She was the personification of his imagination, yet she was here; she was real, in the flesh, dressed in sequined silk.

"Father, please excuse us. Neal and I are going to find a good spot to watch the pyrotechnics."

"Rather early for that, isn't it? You've barely touched your meal."

"Too much caviar and *tortue verte au claire* rests uneasily, you know. Besides, we can barely hear ourselves think! I prefer a secluded place much more conducive to conversation."

"Yes, I'm sure you do. But not too secluded, of course."

"Of course!"

Neal and Katherine made their way out to the veranda. "So, what's your issue with Dr. Akers?"

"He's a cad! And worse, for sure."

"Well, it's evident he likes you!" Neal teased.

"He likes anything with a skirt!"

"Oh, come now. He can't be that bad."

"Oh, you just don't know. Poor girls that work for him never stay long. It's constant harassment with him. And some of the things he does in that office…well, it just wouldn't do to say!"

"Really?"

"Illegal, if you want to know the facts. And his poor wife is oblivious!"

"Shhh," Neal whispered. He nodded toward some people exiting the dining hall and walking out onto the veranda.

Katherine looked up at the banquet attendees as they walked past. She smiled and nodded at them, then turned to Neal. "Let's find another place."

They left the veranda and walked to a small bench on the far side of the lawn.

"So, what were you saying about Dr. Akers?" Neal asked. "He's doing things that are illegal?"

"Yes, and even immoral!"

"No!" Neal teases. "How do you know?"

"Well, first, he's working with those bawdy house owners over in the Happy Hollow district. Probably an owner himself."

"Bawdy house owners? Happy Hollow?" Neal laughs. "Come now."

"You don't have to believe it. One of my dearest girlfriends worked in his clinic for half a year, and she said you just wouldn't believe the trail of soiled doves that trail in and out for inoculations, minor procedures, and opium. Opium! I swear, he hands it out for even the slightest of ills."

"Surely that's erroneous! The senator wouldn't be friends with anyone like that."

"Well, that's the interesting thing. He's not that fond of the doctor, but he includes him in all of his political events. It's almost as if there is some ulterior motive." Katherine pauses for a moment, then adds, "What concerns me is, I'm not certain if it is defensive or offensive."

"A mystery, for certain. I'm sure your father has noble reasons."

"Yes. Truly, I know he does. I just wish he would distance himself."

Neal decided to take the conversation in a different, more personal direction. He asked Katherine more questions about her childhood, family, and friends. She responded with fond memories of her childhood home, family events, and especially the holidays. Her eyes had teared up when she recalled her school friends, mostly Beth McHue, who was her best friend even to this very day. In fact, she had wanted Beth to come to the exposition with her, but her father had told her that, this time, he preferred to keep it a family trip.

Neal quizzed her about her travels, of which she had vast experience. He inquired about her dreams, desires, and views about marriage and children. She made herself vulnerable, answering his questions without restraint or timidity.

Katherine, in turn, asked Neal many questions about his life, family, the Navy. They became engrossed in each other, barely taking notice when the pyrotechnics began, and only paused a moment for the finale.

They talked until just before midnight. "Neal, I must go. Father will be wondering if I've been abducted!"

"Abducted…hmm. Now that's food for thought!"

"Silly! You'd better behave!"

"Behave is all I've done. Where's the excitement in that?"

"Oh, stop it! You know you couldn't be anything but a gentleman. And I find it refreshing. Anyway, the gentleman you are quite adequately holds my attention. I think you're the most well-behaved suitor I've ever met."

"So, I *am* a suitor, am I?"

"Yes, I would say so. I hope so." She paused. "I—I find

you truly thrilling."

Neal smiled as he gazed into her eyes. "I have no words to express how I feel just now…or for the entire evening." Neal combed her hair with his fingers, then gently brushed the curls from her forehead. She reached up and took his hand in hers, pulling it to her lips for a soft kiss. Neal glanced around and saw no one watching, but too many too near to risk a real kiss. He looked back into her eyes. "I need to see you again. This night has been amazing, but I need more. I have to see you again."

"We're staying a few days at the Hotel Chamberlin. Father has meetings, and Mother just wants to shop. I can meet you anytime you want."

"I'll have to see what free time I can get. Right now, we're just training and prepping for departure, so the schedule isn't very strict. The officers know we're soon to have long months at sea, so they are rather lenient."

"Do find time," she pleaded. "Anytime, and I'll meet you. Just notify the concierge at the hotel, and he'll get the message to me. They all know Father."

Neal found time; he *made* time to see Katherine. They spent hours together as often as possible, talking, touching, savoring the sweetness of every moment. Katherine managed to convince her father to allow her to stay with her aunt in Newport News for an extended vacation. "Nothing to do with the young sailor, I'm sure."

Katherine and Neal spent the next several weeks developing a deep and meaningful relationship. They shared the experiences of their past, the joys and disappointments of the present, and their dreams for the future. Their time spent teasing, laughing, playing, and loving seemed to speed past. The moments apart, saturated with longing for each other, drug by eternally slow. Underlying every second was the realization that the time was nearing when Neal would have to board his ship and begin the long, long journey, the journey remembered in history as the voyage of the Great White Fleet.

Chapter 4: The Voyage

The U. S. S. Minnesota was to go to New York on November 28th. In the weeks prior, many of the seamen in Neal's group became ill with the measles. Neal managed to avoid the disease, but the whole group was grounded until the illness passed. The days passed, and the Minnesota cruised on without them. Many of those left behind were deeply disappointed and threatened to desert because they were afraid that they were going to be cut from the Fleet.

On December 6th, 380 of the men were reassigned to different ships. Neal was assigned to the U. S. S. Virginia. He was ecstatic as he was still in the Fleet. This was the reason he had joined the Navy, to be a part of a new era in American naval history.

The Fleet left Hampton Rhodes, Virginia, on December 16, 1907. The widely advertised and aggrandized expedition embarked with all the splendor and revelry predicted, including a send-off from the president himself. Neal departed in conflict, excited about the adventure ahead of him but in agony about leaving Katherine behind.

They agreed that he would send a letter or postcard from every port of call. He sent her a card from the island of Trinidad in the British West Indies.

Katherine,

We dropped anchor in Trinidad at four bells on the twenty-third. On Xmas Eve we had a swimming party in the harbor beside the ship. Crazy, huh? On Xmas day, we had a fine dinner, and it was payday. Leaving here in a couple of days to go to Rio de Janeiro, Brazil.

Miss you.
Neal

Katherine followed the Fleet in the news. There was much good press about it, and excitement was still high. The newspaper had a drawing of their progress so far and included the location of their next port of call. There was only slight mention of any issues or AWOL sailors.

A couple of weeks passed before Katherine got another card; this one included a letter.

Katherine,

Hope all is well with you. Seems like a long time since I left your side.

We had an initiation the other day. All of us who had never crossed the equator received a summons from Neptune Rex. It was in his own handwriting. It read as follows:

Domain of Neptune Rex.

You are hereby summoned to appear before his Royal Highness, Neptune Rex, to show cause why you should not be barbered, doctored, butchered, and otherwise maltreated. And also baptized in the water of his Majesty's Domain.

Neptune Rex,
Sovereign of the deep

When the day came, Neptune Rex and his party arrived about 9:30 a.m. He and his bride came in on a carriage with a high seat pulled by four of his party. He was wearing a long white gown, and his long golden hair was down to his waist. His beard was the same kind and length. The whole party wore hideous costumes. Without getting into the details, I have to say it was a terrible initiation. Many seamen were hurt. My right shoulder was injured, but I got over it in about a week. Many men were angered by the initiation; some even wanted to desert. A few didn't return to the ship when we left Trinidad.

We made it to Rio de Janeiro, Brazil, today. I thought it was the prettiest land I had ever seen. There was a tall mountain covered with strawberries and a few tall coffee trees, and another mountain spotted with patches of banana trees, then white rocks, then ditches running the entire length of the mountain. On one side was a lighthouse that looked impossible to get to. At the bottom of the mountains was a white sand beach.

We entered the harbor, where a bunch of Brazilian ships saluted us. On each side was a fort, and beyond them were two more forts. The harbor is about ten miles long and three miles wide and filled with very rough banks. There was every sort of ship and small vessel filled with people in the harbor watching us come in. The main city is on the west side, and houses sit all over the hills. Behind them are tall mountains everywhere. The hospital and prison are on the east side. Every little island of any size has at least one building on it. It is beautiful.

It rains almost every day of the year in Rio. I couldn't go ashore because they had smallpox in the city, and my vaccination was not old enough. I rode around the bay some in a cutter. It was very nice.

Oh, I'm helping the doc some now. Learning a lot.

Must go now. I have bent your ear quite enough.

Wish I could see you.
Neal

Over time more cards came. Neal told of some sites in Chile—the narrow, mountainous Straits of Magellan and of the white houses with red roofs covering the side of the mountain at Punta Arenas. The bay at Valparaiso was as smooth as a lake and had a huge welcome sign made of large white letters laying on the grassy hillside below the fort. The city had a modern streetcar line that served the town and a railroad line that ran way out into the countryside.

He enjoyed watching the sea lions and flocks of birds as the Fleet entered the harbor at Callao. There, the American ships were visited by the president of Peru, who passed and saluted from his own official cruiser. The city beyond the harbor was beautiful and surrounded by mountains. Neal was able to go ashore in Callao and saw many sights, his favorite being the produce market along the wharf. He took a car to nearby Lima, the capital city of Peru. He saw the government prison, several churches, the fairgrounds, the bullfighting ring, and several parks. He described his favorite sight as—

A monument standing in the middle of the street and is about seventy-five feet high. It is a man riding a dapple-gray horse. The horse is standing on his hind legs, and the man has a long spear in his hand, and in the other, he holds the reins.... There were about twenty-five buzzards sitting on top of it.... In some way, I thought this funny.

Scattered here and there in Neal's letters were accounts of poor conditions aboard the ship and the officers' harsh treatment of the sailors. Many times, they were called to quarters to hear court-martials read out, and sentences passed. At every stop, there were sailors abandoning the Fleet.

Katherine was disheartened. This was not the journey they had envisioned. She felt some relief when he wrote of passing through the Straits of Magellan and his time spent in Callao and Lima. At least for a while, he was able to escape the misery and shift his focus to something more positive.

His descriptions were vivid enough to make Katherine feel like she was by his side, sharing the experiences with him. She longed to see him. But she couldn't help but wonder if this voyage was changing him, making him more pessimistic and bitter. She had to dismiss the idea. She told herself she was just being silly. Besides, if she believed it was true, it would be too much for her to bear.

The fleet was scheduled to arrive in San Francisco on May 6, 1908. Neal promised to send Katherine a card from there before taking the long journey across the pacific. This next stretch of the voyage was to take weeks on end with no communication with anyone beyond the ships in the Fleet.

Along the northernmost coast of Baja California, Neal was on deck, as were many other sailors, watching the land pass in the distance as they neared the U. S. border. The peacefulness of the moment was interrupted by a faint scuffling sound. He turned his head to get a better listen; and heard it again. It sounded like it was coming from the seaward side of the ship. He made his way across the deck toward the forward guns. As he rounded the gun turret, he spotted the commotion; three seamen were scuffling with a petty officer.

He knew these guys. He'd crossed paths with them many times on the ship, and they were rough characters. He only knew them by their first names, but that was enough. Buck was the tallest and was downright mean. David was sneaky and cunning; he would get what he wanted by any means necessary. Robbie was scrappy but simple-minded. He was a follower who trusted blindly, and he worshipped that scoundrel, Buck. But the officer...Neal couldn't identify the officer. He saw the uniform but never saw the face.

Neal ran to give aid, but just as he neared the group, he saw Buck pick up a pipe and strike the petty officer in the head. The officer fell, blood rushing from a large gash across his temple. Neal tried to push them away, but the sailors were too much for him. They punched and kicked him without mercy, then threw him over the deck rail. He plunged deep into the salty brine. The eastern Pacific in the late spring was surprisingly cold, cold enough to shock his consciousness into action.

He resurfaced just in time to hear the deserters splash into the water to his left. He scrambled around, trying to locate them and trying to determine the closest route to the shoreline. He got a glimpse of a couple of life rings floating on the water, the closest being just a short swim to his right. The deserters must have thrown them overboard before the petty officer tried to stop them. Neal had to get to one before they did, or he would have no chance. He knew he had to distance himself from them. They had murdered the petty officer, and he was the only witness.

Neal swam as fast as he could to the life ring. Latching onto it, he took a route that took him away from the others and toward a small arm of the beach. It was a long distance to land. But Neal was a country boy who spent long hours swimming in the creeks, ponds, and lakes of Louisiana. He knew he could make the distance. His only question was *what lived in these waters*. The only way to make it to land was to focus. Stay calm. Swim slow, but swim steady, one stroke at a time.

He alternated between swimming and floating on the buoyant water to maintain his intended course. After what seemed like hours, he dragged himself onto the sand, exhausted but alive. It took just a few minutes to regain his wind and his instincts. He knew he had to find the three thugs before he became their next victim. His arms felt like lead weights. With all the strength he could muster, he pushed himself up into a sitting position, knees folded and thighs resting on his calves. He raised up onto his knees and scanned the beach for the others. He saw two of them, just dots on the shoreline about a mile down the beach. Alarmed, Neal wondered, "Where's the third?"

He looked to all sides, hoping the other had not landed close to him. He checked every place the man could be, but to no avail. He searched the shoreline again where the other two landed. Then he saw it—the body floating in the surf. Of course! Neal had the third life ring. The others must have refused to let him share a ring, to drag them down. Satisfied that he was in no immediate danger, Neal rolled over onto his back and rested.

After his lungs recovered and his head cleared, he realized that it would be dark soon. He must find a hiding place for the night. But that could be hard in this semi-arid region. Neal left the beach and found some fallen brush and mesquite in an alcove at the base of a hill. Adding a bit of driftwood, he fashioned enough of a shelter to sleep under, hoping its position in the alcove would be enough to keep him from being noticed.

The desert gets cold at night, making it hard to sleep without a blanket. But Neal was restless anyway, and his mind raced. *Where am I? Where will I go? Is there a town nearby? Would anyone there speak English? I know the border is north, but how far? If I make it across the border, then what do I do?* On and on it went until at last weariness forced him to slumber.

Neal woke with a start. He lay motionless, listening to catch any threatening sound.

"What are you gonna do if you find him, Buck?"

"I'll kill him! It's the only thing we can do."

"You don't think he'll wanna join us so we can all get outta here?"

"*Right.* Then we get across the border, and he turns us in, bonehead!"

"Yeah, okay. I get it."

"You just do what I say, Robbie. I'm the boss."

Neal lay motionless as their voices faded into the distance. *Which one of you is the real bonehead?* he thought to himself. *I'm missing too, so we're all considered deserters. And if that officer died, we'll all be wanted for murder!* his thoughts raced. *And if Buck is as smart as he claims to be, he'll tell Robbie to blame me for it. They'll both blame me for it. One man's word against two. Why would anyone believe me?*

He waited for the two to move away. As soon as he thought it safe, he peeked out to see if he could find them. As luck would have it, he spotted them as they rounded a dune and walked into a cove. When they were out of sight, he crawled out of his cover and stretched his sore, bruised muscles. *So, it's Buck and Robbie I'm against,* he thought. *I just pray I'm smarter than they are.* He gathered his bearings and started across the dunes at the edge of the hills. "North, gotta head north!"

After a half-day of walking, he saw a small desert village. He'd planned on avoiding populated areas, but the need for water forced him to take a risk. He approached a quaint adobe house on the outskirts of town, one that must belong to a farmer. On three sides of the little home were small plots of irrigated vegetables, lush and green. An older Mexican lady stepped out of the side door and made her way to the water well beside the house. Lowering the bucket into the well, she noticed Neal approaching, still wearing his dusty navy whites. She stared at him until he was close enough to address without yelling.

"Americano?"

"Yes. *Sí, sí.* Drink? Water? *Aqua?*" Neal said as he mimicked taking a drink.

"*Agua?*"

"Yes. *¡Sí, agua!*"

"*No! No puedes tomarte el agua....*"

"But I need water! *Agua!*" he said as he mimicked again, but this time with excessive animation.

"*No puedes tomarte el agua. Debes hervirlo. El agua debe hervirse.*" She tried to indicate bubbling with her hands and fingers, but Neal was confused.

"*Debe hervirlo. Americano se enfermará,*" she said, frowning and rubbing her stomach.

"Ah, yes. *Sí.* Sick stomach."

Neal listened as best he could as the *anciana* continued to talk. "*Espera mientras hiervo el agua. Hiervo el agua.*"

The only word he understood was "*agua.*" But when she wiggled her fingers underneath the bucket of water, he understood her sign language; she was going to boil it. "*Sí,*" he said. "*Gracias!*"

He followed her across the yard and up the steps of the house. As she carried the bucket of water inside, he stopped on the porch and plopped down on a short, weathered old bench. He leaned back on the adobe wall, resting in the shade of the rusted porch cover. The shaded adobe was cool on his back, and a pleasant breeze tempted him to nap.

He could hear sounds from the kitchen, the familiar clinking and clanking of someone working at the stove. It made him think of home, of his mom cooking one of her southern meals. He knew he had to get home. Somehow, he had to get home.

Soon, the screen door creaked as she returned with a large cup of water and a plate of flour *tortillas*.

"*Gracias!*" Neal said as he accepted the plate. It was the first time he had thought about food. He rolled a *tortilla* and dipped it into the water, still warm from the boiling. The *tortilla* tasted as good as a steak, and he savored every bite. He found it amazing that something so simple could be so satisfying!

After getting his fill of *tortillas* and water, the woman gave him a stack of *tortillas* wrapped in a thin cotton cloth and an old tin drum canteen, appearing to be of Mexican Army issue. It was full to the plug and warm to the touch. Neal knew it was good to drink and would last a day, maybe two. She also gave him a change of clothes, a nice set that must have belonged to her husband or son. It was great to get out of the navy whites, and it made him less obvious too. Thanking the *anciana*, he set off to the north, hoping to cross the border before dark.

Nightfall came, and Neal found a place to rest by some deadfall cactus under a mesquite tree. In the distance, he could see the lights of some sizeable village, a town maybe, the name of which he had no clue. Was he still in Mexico? Had he perhaps crossed some unmarked region of the border? He would check out the village tomorrow. He fell into a deep and restful sleep.

He was jarred awake by the braying of a *burro*. Sitting up in the sand, he shaded his eyes from the sun, already high above the horizon.

"*Ah, señor!*" someone called. Neal spun around and saw a Mexican standing by a couple of pack *burros*. "It is not safe here in the desert. Rattlesnakes and biting insects everywhere. And thieves!" Neal shaded his eyes from the sun, still trying to adjust to the brightness of the morning. "My name is Maximiliano, the greatest among the traders! I travel from Mexico to California, California to Mexico. If you need it, I can get it!"

"Information?" Neal asked.

"Ah, *información*! What it is you wish to know, *señor*?"

"Where is California? How far?"

"You see that village in the distance? That is Tijuana, Mexico. Beyond that is the city called San Diego, named in honor of the Spaniard San Diego de Alcabá. It is in California, so you have not so far to go."

"Hallelujah! I'll make it by dark!"

"Maybe so, maybe not. But either way, stay along the coast, *señor*. Americanos are not safe in parts of Tijuana."

Chapter 5: Beth McHue

A heavy downpour kept Katherine confined to the house all morning. A hem had come loose in the cuff of one of her blouses, so Subie, the housemaid, had mended it and returned it for her inspection. As usual, Subie's workmanship was excellent. Katherine hung it, as well as a few other items, in her Louis XV walnut wardrobe, which was just a few months older than she. Her father had ordered it from France when he learned he was to be a new father. It was in wonderful condition, large and hand-carved with the traditional French motif of the late nineteenth century.

After catching up on some of her reading, she took a break for refreshment, a light menu typical for a Saturday lunch. The rain had stopped by early afternoon, but a heavy, shrouding mist obscured anything beyond the perimeter of the expansive yard.

Foul weather had always made Katherine sleepy. She reclined on her chaise longue, sluggish from nourishment and weary from the boredom of the morning. The four-poster bed was much more inviting, but her mother was averse to anyone in good health wrinkling the sheets during daytime hours. She hadn't realized she had dozed off until Subie knocked on the door.

"Miss Katherine?" She knocked again. "Miss Katherine, you decent?"

Struggling to awaken, Katherine managed to sit up. "Yes, Subie. What is it?"

Subie opened the door just wide enough to peer through. "Miss Katherine, you have a visitor downstairs. Miss Beth McHue."

"Okay, send her up, Subie. She knows the way. You may leave the door open."

"Yes'm," Subie replied.

Beth was Katherine's best friend since childhood. There had been several "best friends," but Beth was the one whose friendship had lasted, had been the most genuine and loyal. Her father was an attorney and had been one of the senator's closest friends for as long as either of the girls could remember.

Katherine walked over to her dresser and straightened up her hair. Through the open door, she heard Beth's muffled footfalls as she ascended the runner-covered, hardwood steps. She laid the brush on the dresser and turned toward her bedroom door. There was a faint knock, "Katherine?"

"Come on in, Beth." As soon as Beth entered the room, Katherine knew there was something troubling her. "How are you?"

"I'm fine," she replied with a strained smile.

"Beth, you're my best friend. You know I can tell when something is bothering you."

Beth's feigned smile faded from her face. "I just need a friend, Katherine. I need someone to talk to."

Katherine rushed to her friend, seized her by both hands, and led her to the couch. "Here, sit down. What on earth is wrong?"

Beth kneaded Katherine's hands as if she were wringing her own. Her chin quivered as she stared at the floor. "I'm scared!"

"Oh, my dear! What is wrong?" Beth became weepy and found it hard to speak. Katherine sandwiched both of Beth's hands between her own and tried to console her. "It's okay. You're here with me now. You are completely safe," she reassured. She placed an arm around Beth's shoulders to lend some measure of comfort.

After she collected herself, Beth began, "I think I witnessed something illegal at Dr. George's office yesterday!"

Katherine placed her other arm around Beth and patted her on the back as she pulled her close. "It's okay, Beth. You'll be okay," she repeated. "I hate that you had to see whatever it was you saw. I know it had to be traumatic," she sympathized. Then she added with contempt, "But I'm not surprised. Don't you believe for an instant that you're the first to witness that man's devilment."

Beth looked up at Katherine. "Maybe not. But I saw them. I saw them, and I heard them!"

Whatever it was, it had a debilitating effect on Beth. Katherine decided to put her distaste for Dr. George behind her and focus only on Beth and her feelings. "Okay. Take your time, take a deep breath, and tell me just who and what it was that you saw."

Beth sat up, took a moment, then began to recount the events that occurred that afternoon at the clinic. "It was closing time, and all afternoon I had been extremely busy reconciling the clinic financials, so busy that I hadn't even been able to take care of other things. I put away all my paperwork and, well, to be honest," Beth placed a hand on Katherine's forearm, "I *really* had to pee."

Katherine laughed, "I've been there, sister!"

The connection somehow offered Beth a bit of comfort, taking the edge off her anxiety. "We have indoor toilets at the clinic, you know, but the one for the office staff was out of order. My only choice was to go to the one in the clinical area, and, as you're well aware, Dr. George has a conniption any time an office employee sets foot in the clinic. But I had no choice."

Katherine nodded, "Of course!"

"Everyone had gone for the day except Dr. George and me, so I thought I could sneak to the back and relieve myself without being noticed. So, I carefully opened the clinic door just wide enough to slip through and left it open so as not to make any noise. As I tiptoed down the hall, I heard some voices coming from the door of an exam room, the exam room I was about to pass. I froze like a mannequin, hoping I hadn't been heard.

"Then they began raising their voices. It sounded like they were having a disagreement about something. And then I heard Dr. George say something like, 'Tell him he'd better get it right or else—,' but I couldn't understand the rest of the sentence."

"That sounds serious!"

"I know! Then, I don't know what possessed me, but I had the strongest urge to see who Dr. George was talking to. So—"

Katherine sat erect and blurted, "You didn't!"

"I *had* to see! I don't know why, but I just *had* to." Katherine gasped and threw her hands up to cover her mouth. Beth proceeded, "I crept to the very edge of the doorway and stopped with my back pressed against the wall. I was shaking so that I was afraid they would hear my hairpin pecking on the wall."

Katherine blew out a single nervous gust of laughter, then caught her breath. "I'm sorry!" Beth recognized the humor in her own comment and grinned. "What did you do?"

Beth leaned forward as if reenacting her movements. "I leaned over to peek in. The door was mostly closed," then she spun to face Katherine and said in a voice barely louder than a whisper, "but there was enough of an opening that I could see them, Dr. George and a *fiendish* looking man. He was just awful! And a huge stack of money!"

"Money?"

"Yes, bundles and bundles of it, in stacks on the exam table." Beth paused as Katherine gasped. "Then the man…, oh, he was sinister! He gave me chills!" Katherine's eyes grew so wide it seemed they would pop out of their sockets. Beth continued, "He took handfuls of the stacks and put them into a satchel. Dr. George said something under his breath, and the other man said, 'Just remember—keep the money coming on schedule, or your patients may need to look for another doctor.'"

Again, Katherine quickly covered her mouth with her

hands and just as quickly threw them into her lap and leaned toward Beth. "Oh, Beth! What did you do?"

"I wet myself!"

"Oh, how horrible," Katherine managed to say before laughing.

"And then I got out of there!" Snickering, she added, "Probably left a trail all the way out!"

Both ladies had a good laugh, and it seemed to give Beth some relief. Katherine was glad to see her friend's gloom recede, but she also knew the issue was far from over. When their laughter subsided, she asked, "I hate to bring this up, but do you think they saw you?"

Beth pondered the question for a second before responding, "You know, I worried about that. But I don't believe they did. They were too fixed on each other—and the money. If anything, they may have heard me leave."

"Did Dr. George know you were the only clerical person still in the office?"

"No, he leaves through the back door. Only comes to the business offices occasionally during the day. Apparently, the back door is how the hoodlum entered. I'm sure he didn't come through the front!"

"You would have remembered that!"

"Absolutely!" Beth paused for a few seconds. "I didn't go to the office today."

"What?"

"I sent a note with a courier. I said that I was ill."

Katherine realized that she had been so caught up in Beth's story that she hadn't considered the fact that if Beth wanted to continue her job, she would have to return to the scene of the incident. "What are you going to do? Are you going back?"

Despondent, Beth stared at the floor. "I don't think I can."

"I know, it's okay," Katherine said, consoling Beth with a warm hug.

"I mean," Beth sat up again, "something bad is going on, and I don't want to get caught in the middle of it. And if that fiendish man comes in again—" she shakes like a dog shaking water out of its coat. "Oh, he just makes me shiver! I don't think I could keep my composure."

"Darling, don't you worry. You don't have to go back there. Just send Dr. George another note saying that you've been under a lot of personal stress lately, and you think it is in the best interest of your physical and mental health to make a change."

"I think that's a good idea. I really could use a break."

"And you really don't *need* the money," Katherine teased. She knew Beth's father sent her a healthy stipend every month.

"No," Beth responded. Sitting up straight and proud, she added, "But I do like to make my own way, thank you very much!" Both ladies giggled. "I knew I could confide in you, Katherine. Thank you," she said. "You always lift my spirits."

"Of course, dear. I'm just returning the favor." After a quick hug, Katherine shifted her position on the couch, straightened her skirt a bit, then finished by slapping her hands down with a clap on her thighs. "Now. What's next?" she asked.

Beth stared at her for a moment. "What do you mean?"

"I mean, what are you going to do now, after you send the note to Dr. George?"

"Oh! Well, I don't know. My goodness, we just decided that I would resign. Ha! I haven't had time to give it any thought." Beth's gaze darted around the bedroom as if somewhere hidden in the décor was an item that would give her a clue. "I guess," she paused, "maybe—"

"I think it would be a good time for you to go see your family; visit some of your favorite sites in Corsicana. Be rid of this town for a while and just free your mind."

"Oh, Katherine, do you really think so?" She gazed across the room again as if picturing Corsicana, or maybe a joyful embrace from her parents. "I think that is a wonderful idea, just wonderful." She looked back at Katherine. "It would be, wouldn't it?"

"Of course, it would! I think it would be just what the doctor ordered! Please excuse the *calembour*, as the French would say!"

Rolling her eyes, Beth responded, "Pa-lease!" They both had a good laugh.

Chapter 6: San Diego to Houston

Neal trudged on until he reached San Diego. It didn't look too far, but the distance was deceiving, and the trip was hot, dry, and dusty. He walked a lot of the way but also found rides with locals on wagons and *burros*. He sold his navy whites for a few American dollars, which was enough to eat for a few days. But he needed to decide what to do. If he could just get home, his dad could figure this out. But home was a long way off. It would take many weeks to get there by foot, horse, or buggy. His best option for travel was the train, which could take him almost to his family's front door. He had known several families that had ridden the train from Louisiana to San Diego or Los Angeles.

Neal found a job on a farm and worked long enough to earn some travel money. He took the California Southern railway and traveled eastward to Colton, then the Southern Pacific to Yuma, Tucson, El Paso, San Antonio, and Houston.

Houston! His plan was to go to his father for help, but he couldn't bear the thought of leaving Houston without seeing Katherine. He had to find her! But his ticket destination was Gibsland, Louisiana. Would his ticket be void if he didn't continue on the train? He approached the ticket counter and interrupted the busy desk clerk. "Excuse me, sir. Is there a possibility that I can delay the last leg of my trip?"

"What is your itinerary?"

Neal handed him his ticket stubs. "Well, I started in San Diego, and my final destination is Gibsland, Louisiana. I have some business in Houston and need to stay a day or two before going on."

"Let me see here; Gibsland is usually okay. Shreveport is the toughest link on your route, but it's seldom fully booked. Good thing you're not going to Beaumont; that train is always full." The clerk looked over the bookings on the Rabbit line to Shreveport. "Okay, let's see...you may be in luck, son. Looks like the Rabbit reservations for the next several days are light."

"Great!" Neal sighed in relief.

"I tell you what; you just come to talk to me when you're ready to go. I'll make sure you get on the train."

"Thank you so much, sir. I really appreciate it."

"No problem, young man."

Neal turned to walk away. "Oh, one more thing," he said as he turned back to the clerk. "Can you direct me to Senator Joseph Bailey's house?"

The clerk was quick to oblige, and Neal got underway. He took a carriage through the city to the senator's neighborhood. It was a breathtaking place—in the city with all the amenities, but with enough timber to give it the feel of rural acreage. All the homes were magnificent structures on estates of three to five acres, all bordered with ornate, wrought iron fencing. The properties were well-groomed from the street up to and around the houses, with outlying areas often thick with trees and undergrowth. It occurred to Neal that this would be perfect for slipping up to Katherine's house. But there was no way to get on the property before dark without being seen. So, he had to find a place to pass the next few hours.

"Driver, I'm a bit hungry. Is there a café nearby?"

"Yes, sir, about five blocks down."

"That would be great. Just take me there if you don't mind."

"Be glad to, sir."

It wasn't long before the driver stopped the carriage in the middle of a picturesque little shopping area. Neal paid him for the ride and stepped down onto the street. He stood there for a moment, checking out the surrounding shops and stores. There was such a variety here that there seemed to be little reason for the residents in the area to ever leave the neighborhood. Soon, the aroma of fresh bread and coffee from the café grabbed his attention. He walked in and found an open table at one of the street-side windows.

It didn't take long for the waitress to bring his sandwich and water, which he wasted no time in consuming. Since his cash was low, he didn't get dessert but finished his meal with a cup of fresh Arbuckle coffee. He leaned forward, placed his elbows on the table, and gazed out at the passers-by on the street.

He couldn't help but notice the predominance of wealth and gentility. Men in expensive hats and suits, women in flowing gowns and headdresses, all milling about as if they had not a care in the world. Neal wondered what a life of real wealth was like and if he would ever live it. He couldn't see himself living as some do; elitist snobs of inflated ego, living on old family money that they had no part in earning. Maybe he could be of the new money breed, earning his wealth through ingenuity, diligence, and hard work.

Conversely, there were a couple of vagrants within sight, sitting street side, now and again lifting up a hand to beg for a handout from anyone who happened to be passing by. Seldom did anyone stop, and even rarer was the gift of more than a few pennies. Neal questioned which class was the more genuine. But he recalled many of his father's friends who were very wealthy yet remained humble and generous. He felt certain they were in the majority. At least he hoped so.

Pondering the drama outside the café window, he heard a clattering down the street. He turned to see a beautiful palomino horse pulling an ornate, black, four-passenger Studebaker carriage. As it came closer, Neal was shocked to see Katherine riding in the passenger seat. Impulsively, he stood to try to get her attention. He wanted to wave his hands but realized he couldn't risk drawing the attention of the café patrons any more than he already had. The carriage drew alongside the café, and at that moment, Katherine glanced over at the window. Her eyes grew wide as she recognized Neal staring at her from behind the glass. Their eyes met as they had on that warm day in September at the Robert Fulton Day Parade.

As the carriage passed, Katherine leaned forward in her seat and continued gazing at him. Neal timidly raised his hand to assure her that her eyes weren't deceiving her. It *was* him. She turned as if unsure of her next move. Should she acknowledge him or keep riding? Her excitement and curiosity won.

The carriage had barely stopped when she stepped down

onto the street. Neal exited the café and hurried to meet her. As they drew closer, he motioned her toward a small alley between two of the nearby shops. They clasped hands and entered the alley. Katherine spun around and embraced Neal, passionately kissing him on the lips, face, and neck.

"Neal! Neal! I can't believe it! They said you were missing, maybe dead! But you're here! You're here!"

"I had to see you! I couldn't bear to stay away!" They held each other, savoring the moment. "Wait. How did you hear that I was missing?"

"Father gets updates on the Fleet from the secretary of the Navy—as a favor to me. I read them because it makes me feel close to you." She looked up into his eyes. "I read the report that said you were a deserter. I didn't believe it, not ever! Father said he would check into it and see what he could discover, but he always said you were just missing, no further information was available."

"Katherine, we must talk."

"Yes, of course! What happened? Are you okay? Where have you been?"

"That's what we need to talk about. I need to tell you what happened. The truth, not what everyone assumes."

"Neal, what do you mean? What does everyone assume?"

Without warning, the carriage driver called from the entrance to the alley. "Mrs. Katherine, da senator's 'spectin' you home soon."

"Yes, Benjamin. Ready the carriage; I'll be there in a moment."

"Katherine, when can I see you? It's very urgent!"

"Tomorrow. Father has guests tonight, but tomorrow. Do you have somewhere to stay the night?"

"No, but I'll find something. I'll be okay."

"Come with me. You can stay at our house. There's plenty of room."

"No, I can't. No one must know I'm here. I have a lot to tell you."

"The storage house then. Benjamin can find a mattress for you."

"Wouldn't that be dangerous? I mean, Benjamin might…."

"Don't worry about Benjamin; he's loyal and smart. He won't utter a word."

Neal followed Katherine to the carriage. "Nice carriage, though I must admit, I expected the senator to have a fancy automobile."

"Yes, well, he has a Ford Model K, a 1907 model. But I still prefer the Studebaker for my evening rides. It's much quieter."

Neal smiled. "And more romantic."

She batted her eyes and grinned. "Depends on the company."

Neal laughed as he helped her into the carriage. He jumped into the seat beside her and held her hand as Benjamin drove them home. As they approached the house, he asked Benjamin to stop the carriage.

Katherine was confused. "Why don't you want to ride on to the house?"

"That's what we need to talk about tomorrow," Neal replied. "In the meantime, don't tell anyone you've seen me. And that goes for you too, Benjamin."

"Seen who?" Benjamin stared straight ahead from his driver's seat. "I ain't seen nobody nor nuthin'."

"Neal, what's wrong?"

"It's okay, Katherine. We'll talk about it tomorrow. I just want to fill you in on some details about where I've been."

"Sounds ominous!"

"It'll be fine. You just get some rest tonight. Okay?"

"I'll certainly try." She looked over at Benjamin. "Benjamin, can you help Neal make the storage building comfortable for the night? Nothing fancy, just tolerable."

"Yes'm," he replied.

She turned back to Neal. "You get some rest yourself. I think you need it."

"Thank you. I'll see you tomorrow." He kissed her, then took a step away from the carriage.

"Tomorrow," she said as the carriage pulled away.

Benjamin, with Neal's help, set up the storage building as a makeshift hideout and managed to confiscate a pitcher of water and some food from the kitchen. Neal ate what food he could, which wasn't much. He was too nervous to eat a lot. He settled down on the small mattress Benjamin had brought to the office of the storeroom. It was supported by a frame made of old blocks and planks; very crude, but it was adequate and comfortable. He was exhausted, and within minutes he was in deep slumber.

He woke early the next morning, and by the height of the sun, he estimated the time to be around 6 a.m. It was the first full night of sleep he'd gotten in a while. The night had been quiet, and the cross ventilation from the open widows made the temperature in the room quite pleasant. He made breakfast of his evening leftovers and passed the time by reading some old newspapers he found on the dusty desk.

But his thoughts were on Katherine and the story he had to tell her. Would she believe him? Surely, she would. She *had* to believe he was telling the truth. His hope was that she could offer another perspective that would help him decide what to do. He'd learned from his father to value a woman's viewpoint, her intuition. Use it or not, it always helped to have another's input. But the one thing he knew was that asking Katherine's father to help him was risky business. Why wouldn't the senator just turn him in and receive the credit for the capture of an accused deserter and murderer? And Katherine—what would she think? Did he truly care for her, or was he just using her to his advantage? Neal knew he couldn't bring the subject up; it must be her idea. This must be handled correctly, or he would lose her.

It was just after 9 a.m. when Katherine slipped out of the house. She wandered around the yard as if she were just out enjoying a morning stroll but soon made her way to the storehouse. Neal met her as she closed the door, greeting her with a soft kiss and a tight hug. Katherine delighted in both.

"Did you sleep well?"

"Yes, fine." Neal's preoccupation was obvious in his tone.

"Have you had any breakfast?"

"Yes. Benjamin brought me a feast last night, so I ate the leftovers this morning."

"That's good," Katherine replied. "I certainly wasn't going to cook!" Neal smiled and squeezed her tighter. Pleased that she had elicited some emotion in him, she decided to broach the dreaded subject. "What is the urgent topic you need to discuss with me?"

He released his hug and clutched her arms just above the elbows. He stared deep into her eyes. "Promise me you'll hear me out before you pass any judgment."

"Neal, you're scaring me! What is it?"

He gave her a subtle shake for emphasis. "Promise me!"

"Yes, of course. I promise!"

He released her and began to pace. "It's about the journey, the Great White Fleet. Really, it's more about what happened when I left it. I need you to listen, to help me figure it out."

"What is it? What happened?"

"We were all, the seamen, excited about the adventure, the journey we were starting when we left Hampton Roads. It was a joyous time for all of us. But within a few weeks, it became obvious that it would be nothing like we had imagined. I mean, it was exactly the opposite."

"Yes, I read that in your letters."

"Discipline was excessive, conditions were deplorable.

Food was rationed, and we suffered from hunger pains night and day."

"Oh, Neal, I didn't know it was so bad! In your letters, you mentioned that conditions weren't good, but I never imagined it was that bad!"

"I didn't want to worry you. I held hope that when we ported, we would take on provisions, and things would get better. And they did at first. But some of the seamen were so disheartened that when we ported, they would abandon ship. Some would take port leave and never return, and others would leave the ship without permission. Some would even jump overboard and swim to shore. When the commanders heard about it, it would anger them, and discipline would get even worse. Those of us remaining were threatened, sometimes punished."

"Oh, that's horrible!"

"Okay, I really need you to listen to what happened next. This is really important."

"Okay."

"We were cruising the coast of Baja California, within sight of the beach, when I heard a scuffle behind a gun turret. So, I went to investigate. Three seamen were beating a petty officer, so I went to his aid. One of the men took a pipe and smashed the officer's head. He fell. Blood poured profusely onto the deck. I couldn't believe it. Then they jumped me, all three of them, pulling and punching and kicking. I fell into the railing, holding on, trying to stay on my feet. But two of them grabbed my legs and flipped me over the rail. I fell about fifty feet before I hit the water."

"Oh, Neal! You could have been killed!" She wrapped her arms around him and held him tight. After a moment, she leaned back and stared at him, "What did you do?"

"Just before I hit the water, I saw them jump over the rail. The ship was moving at cruise speed, so they hit the water 30, 40, maybe 50 feet from where I went in. I swam away from them as hard and fast as I could. I saw a couple of life rings in the water. I guess they threw them out before jumping. So, I swam over and grabbed the one closest to me and swam hard toward the beach. By the time I got there, I could see two of the men about a mile away, walking out of the water and falling onto the beach. I was afraid the third man was somewhere close to me. But soon, I saw him floating face down in the water."

"Oh, how horrid!"

"Katherine, do you understand where I now stood? There were four seamen missing and an injured petty officer on board. Do you understand?"

"He died, Neal. The officer died." Neal stared at her, trying to process the news. Katherine continued, "Father received a note from the Navy secretary that I wasn't supposed to see."

Neal realized that his situation was much worse than he'd thought. "He died," he repeated. "We're *all* fugitives, wanted for desertion and murder! Even me! As far as the Navy is concerned, I could have killed the officer. And on top of that, I'm the only eyewitness. So even the two living deserters are after me!"

"Oh, Neal, I'm so sorry! What you must have gone through, you poor dear!" She tried to take his face in her hands. He intercepted them in midair and looked at her in earnest.

"Poor dear? Katherine, do you understand how bad this is? I'm a wanted man! I'm considered a deserter and a murderer by the United States Navy! Killing an officer is a death sentence!"

Katherine caught her breath; her eyes widened as she realized the gravity of Neal's position. For a moment, she was speechless. Then, under her breath, she exclaimed, "Mercy me! Neal, what are you going to do?"

He turned and moved a few steps away. "I don't know."

"Can't you go to the officials, tell them the truth?"

He spun around and looked her in the eyes. "Why would they believe me, Katherine? There's no one to corroborate my story except the two seamen, and they'd probably say that I did it so they could get cleared. That makes it two against one. Why would anyone believe me?"

"You're right. But there must be a way out of this!"

"I've given it a lot of thought but have yet to come up with a viable solution."

"Is there anything I can do to help?"

"I would love to hear any ideas you have. My father always sought my mother's input on important matters. She always saw things from a different perspective and proved to be quite wise. Maybe, together, we could come up with something."

"Sounds like your father is wise to go to her. A lot of men have too much pride. I'm the other way around; I always go to my father when I have problems."

"That's good."

"Wait! Father! That's it, Neal! Father can help!"

"Your father?"

"Yes! He's a senator, remember? He knows all the important government and law enforcement officials. And the secretary of the Navy! He can speak to him on your behalf!"

"That's great! Would he do that?"

"Of course, he would!"

"Wait—to do that, he would have to believe my version of the incident. And why would he trust a wanted man?"

Katherine put her arms around Neal and looked at him with sincere affection. "Because he trusts me. And *I* trust you."

They shared a passionate kiss, then held each other for a moment. "Let me go speak to him before Dr. George gets here."

"Dr. George?"

"Yes, you remember that horrid acquaintance of Father's, Dr. George Akers. You met him at the Robert Fulton Banquet."

"Oh, yes, Dr. George Akers. He sat on your left at the table. How could I forget? We had such a wonderful conversation about him!"

"Yes, the dirty old man. I wish Father would dis-friend him!"

Neal laughed at her vehement candor. "Well, why doesn't he?"

"As you recall, I believe there's some agenda there. I believe it is political support. Dr. George has influence with a sector of the wealthy whose money appears to come from dubious exploits."

"Dubious exploits?"

"Yes. Dishonest money, but money, nonetheless. Father doesn't approve of that crowd, and he's not real fond of Dr. George, either. But I learned that Dr. George helped sway their votes to get Father elected. He respects that, whether he likes the man or not."

"And your father legislates softly where they're concerned?"

"Oh, heavens no! He's too honest for that, which will one day be the demise of their relationship, I'm sure. And I'll be glad of it! Anyway, I must go!" Katherine gave him a quick kiss. "I'll be back." As she opened the door, she turned and looked back at Neal. "It may be a while. Father has to be persuaded delicately."

"Good luck!" She smiled back at Neal, then exited the door.

Chapter 7: Due Process

Katherine found her father sitting at his desk in the library, perusing some paperwork. Without speaking, she slipped into the room, careful to avoid any sudden or anxious moves that would arouse suspicion. "Father, are you terribly busy?"

"No, just looking over some documents for a meeting I have in town later today."

"Do you have a moment to talk?"

"I always have time for you, sweetheart." Katherine leaned over and kissed her dad on the cheek. "Thank you!" he said. "I've either done something right, or you want something. What's on your mind?"

"Father, that's not nice." He laughed. After a short pause, she said, "I've been thinking a lot lately about...about Neal."

"Ah, yes. Neal. Have you heard any updates on him? Has he surfaced anywhere?"

"Well, let me ask you a question. What have you heard about his situation?"

"His situation?"

"Yes, Father. You know, about his disappearance from the

ship."

Senator Bailey nods in understanding. "Okay, what have you heard, Katherine?"

"I asked you first! You've kept things from me, haven't you?"

"Katherine, all I've heard is pure speculation. I didn't want to alarm you with something unproven."

"I'm an adult, Father. I can handle the truth. Just because I love him doesn't mean I can't be objective. Isn't that what you've taught me all my life?"

"Yes, but love has a way of veiling one's vision. I'm your father; I don't want to see you hurt."

"But I *am* hurt, Father. Hurt that you didn't trust me with the truth!"

"We don't know the truth."

Katherine collects her thoughts for a moment. "Father, let me ask you a hypothetical question."

"Hypothetical?"

"Yes. They say Neal jumped overboard and that he killed an officer in the process. Is that what you've heard?"

After a short pause, the senator answered, "Yes."

"What if that's not what happened. What if some other seaman killed the officer? What if Neal was trying to stop them and got knocked overboard? Neal would be innocent then, right?"

"Of course, he would. My question is, where did you get

this story? Have you seen Neal?"

"Would you help him, Father? Would you help him with the authorities?"

"You have seen him! Are you hiding him in this house?"

"No! I—I mean, yes, I've seen him, but no, he's not here!"

"Katherine, if you've seen him, it is our duty to turn him over to the authorities and let due process take its course."

"He couldn't get a fair trial! One of the real murderers would have to testify on his behalf, and why would either of them do that? Why wouldn't they just—just blame him to clear themselves? It would be two against one. They could corroborate on a lie!"

"This is military business, Katherine. You're not dealing with a village constable. We can't just walk in and tell them to let him go. There's no proof of his innocence."

"But, Father, you know the proper authorities—the secretary of the Navy, the attorney general, the president even. Can't you talk to them and tell them Neal is innocent, or at least that he deserves the benefit of the doubt?"

"Have you never heard of 'innocent until proven guilty'? Due process *is* giving him the benefit of the doubt. And as a senator, I can't get involved in trying to release someone who may be a murderer. Can you imagine the outcry if that made the newspapers? Look. If you see him again, you must tell him to turn himself in!"

"I can't believe you, Father! You would hang him just like they would!"

"Katherine!"

"Well, *if* I see him again, I'm going to tell him to run. And if he does, I just may run with him!" Katherine stormed out of the library and slammed the door behind her.

"Katherine! Katherine!" She ignored her father's calls and continued up to her room.

Katherine wasn't sure how long she'd been in her room, but she knew she had to wait until she was sure her father wouldn't notice her leaving the house. Neal met her as she entered the door of the storehouse.

"Katherine! I've been worried sick about you. What happened? I expected you back hours ago!"

"I couldn't come straight back, Neal. Father is watching me like a hawk." Her demeanor and the look on her face erased his hope. "He says he won't get involved and that you must turn yourself in, face due process."

"But Katherine—"

"I know, and I *tried* to convince him. Sometimes he can be so stubborn!" They embraced each other and stood in silence, their racing minds shutting down, yielding to the tragedy of their circumstance. After a few moments, Katherine began to calm down. Without releasing him, she said, "We must give him some time, let him mull it over for a while. Sometimes that helps."

"Well, before he has time to mull it over, do you think he'll turn me in?"

"I don't think so. But then, I also thought he'd help you out." Shaking her head, she said, "I just don't know what to think anymore!"

Neal leaned back and looked into her eyes. "I think—I think I can't stay here any longer. He knows I'm seeing you, and you said he's watching you. Maybe he won't turn me in, but maybe he will. I can't take the chance."

"I know." She embraced him again, dreading the inevitable. "But where will you go? What will you do?"

"Maybe I should go to my father. He's no senator, but he *is* a wise man."

"Yes, that's a good idea. He might have a solution. And maybe being in familiar surroundings will help you see things more clearly."

"I certainly hope so." Neal stepped to the window. Katherine stood at his side, holding onto his arm as he peered out to see if anyone was in the yard. "No one in sight. Maybe I should go now."

"Wait until after dark. That'll give me time to get you some food. Oh, and I think you need a hat. It will help change your appearance."

"Okay, I'll welcome the food. And the hat if I must."

"Yes, you must! I insist!" Katherine gave him a quick kiss. "I'll be back, but it might be a while."

"I'm going nowhere," Neal teased. He gave her another kiss, and she exited the storeroom door. He watched through the window as she walked across the side yard to the house. She opened the door to enter but paused to look back at the storehouse. Neal wasn't sure if she could see him through the window, but he waved anyway. She smiled, then turned and entered the doorway.

Just after sunset, Katherine returned with a knapsack. She entered the storehouse then placed the knapsack on a box. To soften the graveness of the moment, she grinned and said, "I have gifts for your journey, sir." Neal smiled. Her attempts to lighten the mood were endearing to him.

She opened the knapsack, reached in, and pulled out a gray, cotton Newsboy hat. "First, we have a nice hat to contribute to your anonymity. A recent Christmas present to Father that he hardly ever wore." She placed it on his head, tilted to one side. "Very stylish. I believe it looks better on you than on Father!"

Neal laughed and played along. "Why, thank you, ma'am."

She reached back into the knapsack. "Second, we have a pocketknife. Father says every good man carries a pocketknife."

"Father is quite correct!"

"And next we have an extra shirt, trousers, and socks. Everyone needs a change of clothes. It's only civilized, you know."

Neal laughs. "No underpants?"

"You'll have to work that one out yourself!" They both laughed.

"Remaining in the bag for you, sir, is food—ham and cheese on a bun for supper, two of them, and a half dozen sugar cookies for breakfast. I'm afraid you'll have to purchase your own beverages."

"Thank you, ma'am! I am truly grateful!"

She slips her arms around Neal's waist, gives him a firm

hug, then looks up into his eyes. "I'm going to miss you—and fear for you. Please write me, let me know what's happening."

"I will, but I can't use my name or anything close." Neal thought for a moment. "Ah, I know! My uncle used to tell a story about a character named James Landis. I'll use that name."

"James Landis. I think I can remember that."

They stood speechless in each other's arms. Neal hated to release her, but he knew it was time. "Katherine, I have to go."

"I know. But I don't have to like it. Please be careful."

"I will." He gave her a parting kiss and a firm hug, then turned to the door.

"Not the door. Go out the back window. I'll close and lock it when you get out. There's a gate in the corner of the back lawn, straight down the fence line outside the window. I'll show you." They made their way to the back of the storehouse. Katherine opened the window and pointed out the fence, then told Neal where to find the gate.

Neal stepped out the window. "You'll hear from me soon."

"Good," she said. "Be careful!" He gave her a quick kiss and turned to make his way to the gate. Katherine called after him, "Neal." He looked back. "I love you!"

His head reeled with emotions. His heart leaped with joy. He smiled, "And I love you!"

Chapter 8: Back Home

The next evening Neal stepped off the Rabbit train at the Southern Pacific Depot in Gibsland, Louisiana. From here, it was less than a twenty-mile walk home. But under the circumstances, twenty miles might take a couple of days. He had to stay out of sight of anyone who might recognize him. He had lots of friends and few enemies, but either way, it would only take one set of loose lips for word to spread that he was home.

The walk was long but went without a hitch. The following day about mid-afternoon, Neal slipped out of the woods and stepped onto the back porch of his family's home. The air wafting from the kitchen smelled sweet, like dessert. He peeked through the screen door and saw his mom, Fannie, standing at the sink, drying the flat pan.

Without opening the door, he spoke, "Mom."

She turned and, for an instant, stood motionless with shock. "Neal! Oh, my Lord! Neal!" He entered the screen door, and she ran to meet him, embracing him in disbelief. "Neal, they told us you were missing. What happened? How did you get here?"

"It's a long story, Ma."

"You look starved! And exhausted! Sit down and let me get you some food."

"Thanks, Ma." As he sat at the table, he took a deep breath. "Mmmm. What's that I smell?"

"Cookies. I just baked some sugar cookies. You want some? And some milk?"

"Sounds great! Been a long time since my last cookies and milk."

Fannie set a whole plate of cookies on the table, then served up a pint jar of fresh milk. She sat at the table with Neal. For a moment, she sat watching, smiling as he devoured the food. "Slow down—you'll make yourself sick!"

Neal nodded his head then looked at Fannie. "It's *so* good to be home."

"Where did you get that Newsboy cap? That's fancy!"

"Ha!" Neal picked up the hat and admired it, turning it from one angle to another to show her all sides. "Well, I lost my navy cap. Just picked this one up along the way." Neal held it out to her, "You want to see it?"

"No," she said. "I don't believe it's quite my style." Neal smiled; Fannie didn't.

Some mothers seem to have a gift when it comes to their children. A way of somehow understanding things that aren't spoken. Fannie had that gift, and she knew something wasn't right. She asked, "Are you in trouble, son?"

He looked at her for a moment trying to choose the best approach to her question. "Who told you I was missing?"

"Sheriff Currie. He's been here a couple of times over the last two or three weeks. He told your dad to be sure to let him know if you came home or made contact somehow."

He finished the mouthful of cookies. "Is Dad here? I need to tell you a story, but I'd rather talk to both of you at once."

"No, but I expect him anytime. He had to go to the courthouse to file some plat maps and survey notes."

"How's his business going?"

"Good. Between the timber companies and the state, he can barely keep up. Your brother Albert works for him now, and they have four chain boys. I'd just love it if you could—"

Neal jumped up from the table. "Shhh! I hear a horse on the road! Check to see if it's Dad. Don't tell anyone else I'm here!"

Fannie ran to the door in time to see Richard turn the horse off the road and head to the barn. "Neal, it's your father." She ran out to the barn to make sure Richard came on to the house as soon as possible.

Little time passed before Neal was able to sit down with Fannie and Richard and tell them the whole story. He began with the first hint of abuse on the voyage and covered every incident from Hampton Roads to Tijuana. He gave a detailed account of his scuffle on the ship, swim to Baja, and subsequent journey home. All he wanted now was to clear his name.

"It's gonna be hard to do that, Neal, unless one of the culprits backs your story. And we don't know if they've even been caught. As it stands now, you're all missing, and there's a dead officer. I'm afraid it's just your word against the evidence."

"So, what do I do, Dad?"

"I'll have to ponder it. Stay out of sight for now. And don't contact anybody."

"Yes, sir. Can I stay here?"

"No!" Fannie flashed a hard look at Richard. "Well, at least not in the house. Sheriff Currie has already been here asking questions, and I'm not gonna be arrested for harboring a fugitive…. Just don't tell me if you sleep in the woods or the barn or something."

"I understand. Thank you."

The conversation lasted until late in the night. Neal told of his experiences on ship and passing through the Strait of Magellan. He talked of sightseeing on the island of Trinidad in the Caribbean, in Rio de Janeiro, Brazil; Punta Arenas, Chile; Callao, Peru; Magdalena Bay, Mexico. Then he described his march up the Baja and the train ride across the American West. Fannie and Richard updated Neal on all the family members, the family surveying business, and local gossip. Neal bid them good night and exited out the back door. He was exhausted but at peace.

Around mid-morning on the third day after his return, Neal sat at the kitchen table where Fanny had put him to work churning milk to make butter. Richard stepped in from the hallway. "You better step into the woods, son. Sheriff Curry is riding this way."

Neal slipped out the back door and crept behind the barn, waiting for the chance to get to the woods unseen. Fanny assumed the churning duty.

As the sheriff rode into the yard, Richard stepped out onto

the porch. "Mornin', J. E."

"Mornin', Richard." He removed his hat and wiped his brow with his shirt sleeve. "Looks like it's gonna be another hot one."

"Sure does. Ol' Bullet's lookin' good."

"Yeah; slowin' down some. Ain't as fleet as he used to be, but he's smart as ever!"

"Ha! Same as us, J. E.! When fleet goes, wisdom grows. I guess that's a redeeming motto for us old guys." As the sheriff dismounts from ol' Bullet, Richard asks, "Have a cup of coffee?"

"Sounds good. Fannie makes the best around."

Richard got them both a cup, and they settled into a couple of old chairs on the porch. They began small talk about the heat, crops, business, and the goings-on around town. The sheriff sipped the last of his coffee and stared out across the field by the road.

"Richard, young Sam Poland says he left his fence gate open a couple o' days ago. Milk cow got out, went into the woods. When he went to fetch her, he said he saw someone out there. Said it looked like Neal, but he wasn't for sure."

"Hmm. Must'a been somebody else."

"So, he isn't here?"

"No, he isn't here, J. E. Don't know where the boy is, but if I see him, I'll send him your way."

The sheriff got up and mounted ol' Bullet. "Richard, you know if I see him, I'll have to arrest him. It's my job."

"I know, J. E. Sometimes we're forced to do things we'd rather not do."

"Glad you understand. It ain't like Neal to do what they're accusin' him of. Got to be a good explanation."

"Got to be. Thank you, J. E."

Sheriff Curry nodded his head, then turned ol' Bullet toward the road and, with a slight nudge in the flank, started back toward town. Neal watched from the woods as Sheriff Currie rode away. After he was out of sight, Neal slipped back to the house and in through the back door.

Fannie, Richard, and Neal sat and brainstormed, trying to determine his options. Neal told them about Katherine and her senator father. He told them about Katherine trying to get her father to help but to no avail. They talked on for most of the afternoon, but the talk produced no clear options.

Richard stood and strolled through the living room and out onto the front porch. He glanced down the road toward town just in time to see three men dart into the woods across the road. They were too far to recognize but close enough to tell that they weren't locals. They appeared to be dressed in uniforms, or maybe suits, and not that of the local law enforcement. *Navy! Or Special Agents!* he thought.

He opened the front door and hurried through the house. Nearing the kitchen, he spoke in a hushed tone, "Neal! You've got to get out of here! There are officials closing in on the house!"

Neal jumped to his feet and grabbed his Newsboy off the table. Fannie palmed her face with both hands in extreme worry and loss. She watched as both Neal and Richard hurried through the kitchen toward the back door. "Where are you going to go?" she asked.

"I don't know, Mom. Maybe—maybe I'll take the train back to Houston." Neal and Richard ran out the door and headed toward the barn.

"Let's saddle the old nag," Richard said. "If you do want to catch a train, ride to the depot in Logansport."

"Logansport?" Neal questioned.

"Too many people know you around here. You're less likely to be recognized in Logansport." Richard continued, "Cross the Red River in Coushatta, then catch the Rabbit at Logansport. When you get there, sell the horse and tack. You should get enough cash to last you a while."

"Thanks, Dad."

Fannie entered the barn as they were finishing up on the horse. "Neal, take this; it's some food, a change of clothes, and $20 for the road. Stay out of sight!"

"Mom, you don't have to—"

"Just take it. I've been saving it for some reason—this must be it!" She gave him as much of a smile as possible under the circumstances. Neal leaned over and gave her a kiss on the cheek and a firm hug.

"Thanks, Mom." He mounted the horse and turned it toward the barn door.

"Son," Fannie called after him, "write us occasionally to keep us up to date. Use the name...James Landis."

"James Landis?" Neal smiled.

"I don't know; it just came to me."

"Recently came to me too!" When he and the nag reached the barn door, he reached down and shook his father's hand, then slipped out into the warm, humid air of a Louisiana summer evening.

Few words were spoken as Richard and Fannie closed the barn doors and hurried into the house. They waited as the old mantel clock ticked off the seconds, one after another, expecting a knock on the door at any moment. But the knock never came; the visit never happened. Either the agents had seen Neal leave, or they were posted in covert positions, watching the house for any sign of him. Darkness came without incident, so Richard and Fannie retired for the night.

The morning sky was clear and beautiful, clouded only by the tension from the night before. Richard left for work as usual, and Fannie began her normal daily routine. Days passed with no visit from the authorities and no word from Neal.

It took Neal close to a week to make the long ride to Logansport. Staying out of sight slowed his travel and was sometimes downright impossible. Many times, he had no choice but to travel the main roads. But he made it, and as far as he knew, he had garnered no suspicion. He found a secluded spot on the edge of town where he could wait out the night. The stand of trees was only about two acres, but it was thick and cozy. There was a good patch of grass hidden from town, tucked away near the backside of the woods. He removed the tack and saddle blanket and tethered the horse with enough slack to let it graze. It was dusk dark, but there was still enough light to get some boughs for a bed and twigs for a small fire. He didn't need the heat, but the smoke from the fire would keep mosquitos at bay.

He nibbled on jerky and a biscuit while he stared into the flames. The same thoughts came again, the same he'd been mulling over night after night. *How did I get in this mess? If I'd only minded my own business on the ship! How am I going to get out of this?* It always progressed the same way. And it always ended with thoughts of Katherine. How could she help him? Is he putting her in harm's way? Should he just stay away from her and figure this out on his own? But he knew he had to see her, even if it was just to say goodbye. Sleep was difficult, but it finally came.

Daylight comes early in a wanted man's camp. Neal was up with the birds, maybe before; he was too preoccupied to notice. He saddled the horse and left the woods, anxious to get on his way. He had tasks to complete. He reminded himself that he could take his time selling the nag. After all, he could leave Logansport tomorrow, or even the next day if necessary. But the thought of Katherine pulled at him. The sooner he got on the train, the sooner he could see her. So, he wasted no time starting the short trip into town.

Logansport was a small community, so finding the depot was easy. Selling the nag and tack proved a little more difficult. The livery was just down the block from the depot. He did his best 'wheeling and dealing' to convince the owner to buy the nag and tack. The owner was a tough negotiator himself, and he knew the value of horses and tack. He didn't give Neal top dollar, but he was fair and gave Neal a fair price.

Neal had to forge Richard's name on the bill of sale and was relieved when it passed without question. Once the transaction was made, Neal walked back to the depot, bought his ticket, and waited. The train wasn't due in town until 11:30 a.m., so he had about an hour to wait. He sat on a bench in the lobby, pulled his Newsboy cap down low on his brow, and feigned sleep. But he kept his ears tuned to every conversation and was ever watchful of those passing in and out.

Chapter 9: The Suits

The Rabbit was the Rabbit—hot, dusty, and loud. But it moved right along, dropping off passengers and picking up others at the various stops southward. Again, Neal kept a watchful eye while trying to remain inconspicuous. Logansport, Joaquin, Tenaha, and Nacogdoches went without a hitch. Neal began to relax. He was out of Louisiana and well into Texas. By this point, he felt sure he was in safe territory.

The train made the next stop in Lufkin, a cow town of about 2,500 souls in east Texas. Neal watched as several passengers disembarked from his passenger car. He looked out the window at the crowd of people waiting to board. Most of them were men, some with wives and a couple of families. It looked as if there were about a dozen lining up at his car.

Then he saw them! Stepping out of the depot onto the boarding dock were two men in black suits, white shirts, and black ties. His heart jumped into his throat! Special Agents! Neal turned away from the window just enough to obscure his profile. He covered the side of his face with his hand and pulled his Newsboy cap down on his brow. It dawned on him that in this small Texas town, he may be the only soul wearing a Newsboy. Had they seen it? He froze in place, trying to avoid any movement that would draw attention to either himself or the cap.

From under the low brim of his cap, he watched their progress toward his passenger car, inching closer and closer to the entry door until they were no longer visible from his vantage point. The fear and dread were almost more than he could bear. Several seats were open, but Neal hadn't noticed how many. Seven or eight passengers entered the car and filled the empty seats.

"Capacity! Next car, please." Neal nearly jumped out of his seat. The conductor was right beside him. He must have entered at the rear end of the passenger car, walking down the aisle as the seats filled up. He smiled as he stepped past Neal, "I get somebody every day! Keeps the job fun!" Neal just sat up and straightened the Newsboy.

He looked out the window to see the remaining passengers, including the two agents, being diverted to another car. He turned away from the window and went unnoticed as they passed. He almost fainted with relief. What a break! *Thank You, God!* he thought to himself. He turned to watch as they all made their way to the car behind his. The conductor stepped into the car while the passengers waited at the door. Neal leaned his head out the open window as far as he dared. He was trying to monitor the location of the agents, but he didn't see them. Apparently, they had found a seat in the car.

A few moments passed before the conductor stepped out of the door. "Capacity! Next car," he shouted again.

Neal blew out the breath he didn't even know he was holding. The conductor led the remaining passengers further back and entered the next car. It must have had open seats; they all boarded. He was relieved, but he knew it was only a temporary reprieve. Those guys were going to disembark somewhere, and it could be the same Houston depot he was going to. *Even worse,* he realized, *once the train leaves the station, they could pass from coach to coach searching for someone...like me!*

His anxiety surged, but he knew he had to appear calm. His mind raced. *They could be in this car within seconds!* The door from their car to his was only about two rows behind him. If they decided to come forward, he couldn't see them until after they had entered, and they would be standing right at his seat before he could move.

His anxiety soared, and his mind began to race. He was trapped! He had to get off the train. But surely, they would see him jump, and all they had to do was pull the emergency cord and get off too. What to do?

Think, Neal! he told himself. He bent over forward in his seat and took a couple of deep breaths. Then his better reasoning began to take over. Did they even know he was on the train? Maybe they're on another case altogether. Maybe they've never even heard of Petty Officer Neal Crowson. And maybe they're not even Special Agents. Anyone could wear a black suit, white shirt, black tie.... But they sure looked the part; hard, driven, on a mission, intent on finding something or someone. Should he get off the train or stay put and risk it?

"That's a unique hat, sir!"

Neal jerked in surprise. "Excuse me?"

"I said that's a unique hat. I've seen them in ads, but I don't believe I've seen a real one before."

Neal looked at the man sitting beside him, a slender, well-dressed gentleman about Neal's height, appearing to be in his late forties. Scrambling for a response, Neal said, "Well, I'm not from around here, just passing through. It's called a Newsboy cap. They're quite popular in some regions." He took the cap off and handed it to the man.

"Ah, this is nice!" He admired the hat, turning it this way and that. "Would you mind if I tried it on?"

Neal had a sudden thought—this might be a great way to get rid of that hat and change his appearance. "Not at all, go ahead! Let me hold yours."

The man took off his hat and handed it to Neal. He wore a wide-brimmed Stetson, similar to a cowboy hat but not quite as large. It was a nice hat, in good shape, but looked to be an older style. He placed the Newsboy on his head and positioned it at a slight angle. "Feels wonderful! How does it look?"

"I believe you were made for that hat! What do you think?"

"It's lightweight, soft—fits like a glove!" He reveled in the feel of it for a moment, then took it off and offered it back to Neal.

Neal held on to the man's Stetson. "Sir, I think you should keep that hat."

"Keep it?"

"Yessiree! That hat looks great on you and matches your suit to boot! I tell you what I'll do—I'll trade my Newsboy for your Stetson. I've always wanted a Stetson like this," he said, examining the hat.

"Well, I don't know what to say. I—I mean, mine is old. Yours looks practically brand new."

"Yes, but I've admired this style for years. Always wanted

one, but Stetson's are a bit above my budget."

"Are you sure? You're serious?"

"Absolutely. I insist! You look like a new man in the Newsboy. A real country gentleman with style!"

He put the hat back on his head. "Would you mind raising the window a bit so I can see myself?"

"Sure!" Neal turned and raised the window just high enough for the man to see his reflection. The train began to pull away from the depot.

"I believe you're right! I like it!"

"I thought you would!"

"Let me walk up to the front of the car. A friend of mine is up there, and I'd like to get her opinion."

"Sure!" Neal was a bit concerned the woman might think the hat looked silly on a middle-aged man. He kept his fingers crossed as the man visited with her at the front of the car. In a few minutes, he returned to his seat.

"So, what's the verdict?"

"She loves modern styles and said I looked 'sophisticatedly casual.'"

"Ha! Well, it's a deal then!"

"Deal!" They shook hands to make it official.

After a few moments of menial conversation, while enjoying their new look, Neal noticed the man frequently glancing at his lady friend at the other end of the car. Neal asked, "Is your friend up front married?"

"No, but she's had offers, I'm sure. Probably near thirty, I'd guess, quite attractive and from a distinguished family of considerable wealth."

"If you'd like, I could exchange seats with her. Maybe she'd like to be sitting with a friend."

"No, you don't have to do that."

"I don't mind. Besides, I occasionally get motion sickness sitting near the back of the car." Neal winked in jest, drawing a chuckle from his seatmate.

"Alright. I'll ask her." He stood and again walked to the front of the car. Neal watched in interest. Soon the man stood, looked back toward Neal, and motioned him to the front. Neal stood and walked to the front. As he neared the lady's seat, the man introduced them.

"This is Miss Mary Edens, of Corsicana, from the Edens oil family. And Mary, this is—my lands! I don't think I ever got your name."

"Nice to meet you, Miss Edens. I'm Ne—James Landis."

"James Landis! Mary, this is James Landis, the original owner of the Newsboy cap!"

"Well, it's nice to meet you, Mr. Landis. But I must say, I think Ben got the better of you in the hat trade." It was the first time Neal had heard the man's name.

Ben roared with laughter. "Maybe so! It's one of my strengths, Mary. I'm a brutal negotiator! Nearly broke his arm before I got him to agree to the trade. Haw-haw!"

Neal smiled at Ben's mirth at his own humor. He shifted his attention to Miss Edens, "I think I came out well, Miss

Edens. I've been wanting a Stetson like this, and Ben needed a little wardrobe modification."

"Yes, into the twentieth century," she remarked.

"Come now," Ben said. "You talk as if I can't hear. I can assure you my French wardrobes are well stocked with the latest in men's fashion."

"Oh, relax, Ben! We're just having a bit of fun. I do like the hat on you. But who knows, if I'd seen the Newsboy on him first, I might have chosen to sit by him instead of you."

Neal blushed but hoped she couldn't tell. He changed the subject. "Corsicana, that's a nice town. What brings you to Lufkin?"

"A friend of mine lives here. I wanted to visit a bit before going back home. I've lived in Houston since I graduated from finishing school."

The train started with a slight jerk. Mary stumbled into Ben's arms. "I think we'd better take our seats," he suggested.

"That would probably be best," Mary replied. She stepped out into the aisle and headed toward Neal's seat in the back. Ben watched her walk down the aisle for an instant, then turned and smiled at Neal.

"You better follow her," Neal urged.

"I believe I will!" Without pause, Ben joined Mary in the seats at the back of the car.

Neal sat down in Mary's vacant seat. Beside him, a weathered old man was leaning against the window stile. He appeared to have slept through their entire exchange. *Whew,* Neal thought. *Different hat, different seat. Much better chance to avoid the agents if they come this way.*

By this time, the Rabbit was racing down the tracks. Survival was doubtful if a body jumped off at this speed. Neal was here to stay, at least to the next stop, wherever that was. He followed the lead of the old man; he pulled his new Stetson over his eyes and tried to rest. Not sleep, but rest.

The back door of the coach opened and shut with a bang. Neal froze. Through the bumping of the train and the mumbling of the passengers, he could hear hard soles thumping against the wood floor. Up the aisle, they came, drawing closer and closer to his seat at the front. Just as the footsteps reached his seat, a hand landed on his shoulder. "Excuse me, sir."

With his heart beating in his throat, Neal slowly turned and looked up into the face of the conductor.

"Wasn't there a lady sitting here earlier?"

Neal felt immediate relief. "Yes, sir. Um, a friend of hers was sitting in the back, so we traded seats. I hope that's okay?"

"Okay? I'm thrilled! Ha! I thought maybe I was dreaming!" He stood and looked back at Mary. "Ha! I walked right by her." Looking back at Neal, he said, "She's a real looker, you know!"

"Couldn't miss that!" Neal answered. With that, the conductor smiled, then turned and continued his rounds, stepping out the forward door and into the next coach.

Neal melted into the seat with exhaustion, and not because it was a hot summer afternoon on a train in east Texas. *I've got to relax*, he told himself, *or I'm going to worry myself to an early heart attack!* He resolved that whatever was going to happen was going to happen. He just needed to stay calm and do whatever it took to avoid attracting attention.

The next half hour was uneventful. The train started to slow for the next stop, and Neal peered out the window as much as possible around the sleeping old man. They pulled alongside the depot and stopped. The conductor announced that passengers were allowed fifteen minutes to get a drink or use the restroom, but the train was pulling out in twenty, all aboard or not. Most passengers rushed to get off the train. All the noise and commotion inside the car woke the old man. He bent over and grabbed his bag from under the seat, then readied to exit the car. Neal stood and stepped into the aisle to let him out. The old man exited without a word.

Neal decided to stay on the train. Since most of the passengers had gotten out of the car, he dropped his hat on the seat and stood in the aisle, stretching his legs. He put his hands behind his head, elbows in the air, and twisted and turned from one side to the other to work the kinks out of his spine. He straightened up and turned to look out the window. There, on the boardwalk by the depot, stood the two men in black suits.

He snatched up his hat and sat in an empty seat on the other side of the car, the side farthest from the depot. Lowering his hat over his eyes, he watched the men as they scanned the boardwalk in both directions, one looking south, the other north. They were looking for someone, it was obvious. One of them spoke, and they both turned to look south. Neal saw another black-suited man approaching them. They greeted each other with a handshake and a short discussion, then all three turned and walked into the depot.

Was the third man going to join them on the train? Were the two from the train staying here in—whatever this town is? Neal couldn't stand the mystery; he had to have answers. He decided he would leave the train and find them. Then he would watch them from a distance to see if he could figure out what they were up to.

Neal slipped out of the train car and strolled over to the depot. He stood by the window for a moment, standing under the eave as if he was just trying to stay out of the sun. After a few seconds, he strolled to the other side of the window, peeping in as he passed to see if he could get a glimpse of them. No luck. Had they exited the other side of the depot and gone street side? Maybe they caught a carriage or automobile and left the area. It could be he was in the clear.

He decided to go around the depot to check out the street on the other side. He stopped before rounding the corner of the building, leaned against the wall, and studied the pedestrians ahead and to his right—no black suits. He paused a moment, then peeked around the corner on the street-side. Scanning the area as best he could, he again saw no suits. *Whew! I guess this was their destination and they left*, he thought. He stepped around the corner and walked down the sidewalk.

Since he was off the train, he decided that he might as well use the restroom before re-boarding. But he'd better hurry; boarding was about to start. He made his way to the large public restroom on the opposite side of the depot. Just as he reached for the doorknob, the door flew open and bumped the brim of his Stetson. He stopped with a jerk, catching his hat as it fell over his face. "Excuse me, sir," he said just as the brim dropped below his eyes. Pushing past him without a word was a man in a black suit, with two other black suits following him. Neal bent his head over and placed the hat on it with one hand while holding the door open with the other. The men passed without even acknowledging his presence.

Neal stood holding the door, watching the men as they walked toward the street. He decided he'd better go on in, just in case one of them looks back. It would look suspicious if they saw him standing there staring. His mind raced again. *Are they leaving, or just making it appear that they are? Are they waiting for me to leave the restroom so they can nab me? Maybe they're waiting for me to board the train so they can trap me. Do they even know I exist?*

The one thing he knew was that he couldn't stand being boxed in where he couldn't see what was going on. He had to get outside! He left the restroom and looked in the direction where he'd last seen the suits. He saw one of the men just as he passed out of sight around the corner of the livery next door. Where were the other two? He scanned the crowd with no luck. Were the men still together, or had the other two re-boarded the train? Neal was in a quandary about his next move.

Over the din of the crowd, he heard the conductor, "All aboard!"

Guess that's it, he thought. *Back to the train and take my chances.*

Chapter 10: The Yardman

Houston came without incident, except for Neal's anxiety level. Every opening and closing of the coach's rear door made his heart race and his face flush. He kept his Stetson low on his brow most of the trip.

Exiting the car at the Houston depot was another chance for him to be cornered by the agents. It was also another opportunity for him to spot them and move opposite to their travel. He took an unassuming position and scanned the crowd, taking his time, looking at every soul on the platform. Still, no sign of the men with black suits, white shirts, and black ties. He took a deep breath of relief as he appeared to be in no immediate danger. Then again, he learned in sports that when you become complacent, your opponent can sneak up and defeat you. He'd seen it happen many times. Maybe he could breathe a little deeper and move a bit more freely, but he had to remain vigilant.

After about half an hour of surveilling people around the platform, Neal decided it would be safe to move about. It was mid-afternoon, and he was starved, so he found a small café not far from the depot. He picked up a map of the city at the counter and looked over it while he ate. The map had a legend that listed parks, landmarks, and major buildings. He remembered Katherine's address and found it, then noticed a site marker on the map, which looked to be just a few blocks past the senator's house. He looked up the number in the legend; it was listed as Watson's General Mercantile. Great place for anyone to be going.

After finishing the sandwich and water, he hailed a carriage and directed the driver to Watson's. "At least two general stores are closer, sir."

"That's okay. Watson's was recommended by a friend."

"Yes, sir. It's a fine store."

They wound through the city, turning this way and that until they got on a larger, better-maintained street. The going was smoother, but the traffic was busy. Soon they turned off the main road and into the upper-class residential area Neal recognized to be Katherine's. The long ride seemed to take forever, though he sensed it was just over half an hour. Soon he saw Senator Bailey's home just ahead.

"Here! Let me off here!"

"Here, sir? We're still eight blocks from Watson's."

"Yes, right here. My legs are cramping; I need to walk."

"Stretch for a bit, sir; then I'll carry you the rest of the way."

"No, I think I'll walk to Watson's."

"Yes, sir. Whatever you wish." The driver steered the horse to the curb and stopped. Neal paid the man and stepped down from the carriage. He strolled down the sidewalk as the horse plodded ahead, waiting until they turned the corner and moved out of sight to make his move. He darted into the woods along the fence line, heading toward the back gate of the Bailey estate. It was just a short distance before reaching the storage building on the other side of the fence. He prayed the back window was still unlocked so he could slip inside without being seen.

Neal slipped through the woods like a fox, appreciating the lessons in stealth he learned while tracking wild game as a youth. The reverie was so pleasant that he began to play the part of the hunter or the tracker, enjoying this clandestine trek to his secret destination. As he neared the back gate of the property, he froze. *Something moved!* He stood motionless, trying to avoid detection. There it was again—movement behind the shrubs. Careful to make no sound, he adjusted his stance to get a clearer view. It was one of Senator Bailey's landscapers trimming the shrubs near the gate.

The only option now was to wait for the yardman to finish and move on. Neal held his position for several minutes, then found a spot nearby that would lend better cover. He waited until the man was facing the opposite direction, then crept the few feet to the thicker undercover and knelt for the wait. From this vantage point, he studied the man for any sign that he may know of Neal's presence. If he did, he was good at hiding it; he made no stops to listen, no repositioning, no subtle glances.

After about twenty minutes, the yardman finished trimming the shrubs, picked up his tools, and walked toward the tool shed on the opposite side of the backyard. He disappeared into the shed. Neal snuck a bit closer to the gate, then waited again, not wanting to risk getting caught while passing through the gate. It was just a few minutes before the man exited the tool shed and walked out of sight on the other side of the big house. Neal felt that it was safe to move. He slipped through the gate and through the small stand of trees along the fence line.

In just a few short moments, he reached the back of the storage building. He checked the window—locked! Now what? He tried again, thinking, hoping that it was just stuck. He stood in front of the window to give it a firm push when he saw someone move inside the dark room!

He spun around and stood beside the window, back to the wall. Had they seen him? He made very little sound the first time he tried the window and hadn't had time to even start his second attempt. So maybe they didn't notice. But how could they not? Even if they had their back to him, wouldn't they have seen a change in the ambient light in the room when he stood in front of the window?

He crouched behind some brush at his side and hoped it was enough to hide him. Staring at the window, he waited to see if someone would peer out, trying to see what or who had peeked in. Suddenly he heard a soft call, "Sir! Sir, it's Benjamin!"

Neal stood up, meeting Benjamin's gaze.

"Sir, I seen you through da glass. You here to see Miss Katherine?"

"Yes, Benjamin." Pointing to the storage building, he added, "I was going to slip in through the window, but it's locked."

"Wait right here; I'll unlock it." Benjamin turned and went back around the building. In a moment, he was at the window, unlocked it, and opened it up. "C'mon, sir. I'll help you in."

"Thank you. I think I can manage it." Neal climbed in with

slight help from Benjamin. He stood up and, with his hands, pushed his hair out of his eyes and brushed off his clothes.

"You hungry? I can bring some food."

"Not too hungry, but thirsty. Mainly I just want to see Katherine."

"Don' you worry at all, sir; I can manage both."

"Thank you. But don't rush! We don't need to arouse any suspicion, you know."

"Yasser, I understand. I'm smart, you know!"

Neal chuckled. "Yes, sir, Katherine told me so!" With a handshake of sincere appreciation, Neal added, "Thank you, Benjamin!" Benjamin smiled and nodded, then sauntered out and closed the door.

Neal watched as Benjamin strolled across the yard. He stopped, picked up some twigs that had fallen out of a tree, broke them into short pieces, and spread them under a shrub as mulch. Neal was amused at his placidity under the circumstances. Then he stood and scanned the yard for any other distractions. Not finding any, he turned and continued his walk to the house.

The old mattress was still in the room as before. After all, it hadn't been that long since he'd gone to Louisiana. However, it appeared to have new sheets; maybe Benjamin had been expecting him all along. Neal smiled at the idea. *Smart man,* he thought. *Smart, smart ole man!*

He sat on the makeshift bed and waited. About half an hour passed when he heard the door open. He jumped to his feet and hid behind the office door just in case it was the senator or one of the hired hands. He hoped for Katherine, but when he peeked around the doorframe, he saw Benjamin entering with a box.

He closed the door then turned with a smile. "Food and water, Mr. Neal." That was the first time he used Neal's name; he must have talked to Katherine.

"Thank you," Neal said as Benjamin carried the box over to the office desk. "When is Katherine coming?"

"Direc'ly! Pro'lly 'round dusk dark." Benjamin opened the box and stepped aside for Neal to inspect the contents. "A bit o' steak, bread, green beans, mashed 'taters, and a quart o' sweet tea. Fit'n for a king! Oh, and a quart o' water for drinkin' or hand washin'."

"Thank you, Benjamin."

"My pleasure, Mr. Neal. It's okay I call you Mr. Neal?"

"Absolutely! You keep taking care of me like this, and you can call me anything you want!"

Benjamin laughed. "Better eat the meat and veggies tonight; da bread will rest 'til mornin'." Then he smiled a big, wide smile. "Gotta go, sir. Wouldn't want a body to miss me. You know, d'ey can't do nothin' 'round here without me!" He nodded his head and gave a slight wave, then turned and went out the door.

Neal nibbled on the food while peeking out the window looking for Katherine. The only sign of life was the yardman putting tools in the tool shed. He was glad the storage shed didn't have as many visitors as the tool shed; if it did, he would constantly be jumping out the back window or crouched in some hiding spot.

He continued to watch out the window. The yardman finally put the last of the tools in the shed. Then he locked the doors and started walking across the yard toward the storage building. Neal wasn't concerned. Odds are he would veer off toward the house to see if the senator needed anything else, then head to the street and be gone for the day. No problem.

But the yardman didn't stop at the house. He continued walking across the yard straight toward the storage shed, giving no indication of veering toward the street. He was coming to the storage building! Neal made a dash to the back window, and as silently as possible, raised it and climbed out. Just as he lowered the window back to the sill, he heard the front door of the storage shed open. He came in and scratched around a bit, obviously looking for something. Then Neal heard him walk into the office and stop, not moving for what seemed like several minutes.

Neal gasped! *The mattress!* he thought to himself. *He's trying to figure out why there was a mattress with sheets on it...and who has been using them. And a half-empty quart of sweet tea on the desk!* Neal was angered with himself for not being more careful. With his back flat against the wall of the building, he stood motionless, awaiting the man's next action. After a few moments, he heard him move; he was continuing toward the door.

The door opened, then closed with a subtle click. Neal waited, but all was silent. He knelt down and looked under the building and out the other side. All he could see from under the building were the yardman's feet. He was standing in front of the door... just standing there, shuffling his feet now and then, but just standing there. Was he going to tell anyone about the mattress, or was he going to dismiss it?

Soon, he stepped away from the building and started walking toward the house. Neal's heart began to race. "He's going to tell the senator!" It was almost dusk dark, so he knew Katherine would be coming soon. What should he do; wait for Katherine or get away now? He looked again, and about halfway to the house, the yardman slowed his pace for a couple of steps, paused, then turned and headed toward the street. Neal drew a deep breath and rolled over on his back. Either the man decided to dismiss the mattress, or he was waiting until tomorrow to report it. At least for now, it was safe to wait for Katherine.

Chapter 11: The Empty Storage Room

The minutes seemed like hours as Neal waited for Katherine. He had always been independent and self-sufficient. Even as a child, he entertained himself as country kids often do, creating his own games, fishing, hunting, exploring, saving the world. But, of course, only after the chores were done. Independence was something he learned from his father, Richard. Yet, he knew Richard was very reliant upon Fannie. He relied on her strength, her wisdom, her alternate view, and her help however he needed it. She was his balance, his confidant, his completion. Neal had never fully understood that—until now. At last, his eyes had been opened; Katherine was *his* completion. She wasn't just convenience, desire, or even lust. He needed her. Neal was surprised at how ready he was to admit that. Need was something new to him. But she filled that need, and he accepted it without question.

The realization of his feelings for her brought him comfort and a sense of security. However, it also presented another dilemma. He now felt genuine concern for someone else's safety and well-being. What would be the repercussions for her if it was discovered that she had hidden him or helped him to escape? Would she be punished by the legal system, or would the senator be able to clear her of any culpability? Neal didn't have a clue. What he did know was that if the roles were reversed, the king's army couldn't stop him from helping Katherine. He had to try to convince her to do the opposite, but he knew the decision had to be hers.

The door opened! Neal froze in horror. His attention had been captured by his reverie, and he hadn't been watching out the window. He sat motionless on the edge of the mattress holding his breath.

"Neal?" It was the soft whisper of Katherine's feminine voice. Neal released his breath and leaned forward over his lap. "Neal, are you here?"

He took a deep breath and replied, "Yes, I'm here." He met her at the door of the office and embraced her in a firm hug. They stood holding each other, neither speaking, both relishing the moment. He relaxed his embrace and looked down at her; she peered up into his eyes. Neal whispered, "You have no idea how much I've missed you."

"Maybe I've missed you more." They both smiled. Neal's eyes shifted to her full, moist lips. The desire in his gaze was obvious, and the want in her soul was overwhelming. She rose to her toes and kissed him intimately, delicately, deeply. She'd never imagined the existence of this depth of passion, much less that she could possess it. It had taken this man, *this man*, to draw it out of her.

As the daughter of a senator, she had met countless men of wealth, power, and position, many of whom had pursued her without any hint of interest on her part. There were a few she had been fond of, but none had ever captured her heart or challenged her resolve. But Neal...Neal was a mystery. Here was a confident man who was capable of being humble, one who never tried to impress her and had demanded nothing of her. Yet his very presence elicited the desire, the need to offer him her heart, her soul, her love. And she knew it was reciprocal; he felt the same toward her. She couldn't explain it; she just knew it. It was inherent, without prompting or pressure. She was his, and he was hers. The very thought of it made her cheeks flush.

"We need to talk. Let's sit." Neal led her to the mattress where she sat, alone.

"What is it, Neal?"

Neal pulled up the desk chair and sat facing her. He took her hands in his and caressed them for a moment before speaking. "Katherine, I'm in a dangerous position. Father couldn't help me with a resolution. In fact, the authorities got a tip that I was in town and came twice to my parents' house while I was there."

"Oh, Neal! What did you do?"

"I had to escape out the back door and hide in the woods."

"How terrible!"

Neal nodded in agreement. "But that's not my biggest concern right now. My biggest concern is you! I don't want you to get into this any deeper than you are now."

"That's nonsense! What makes you think you can stop me?"

"Katherine, right now, you can tell them I came by to talk to you, and you told me to leave. They could never prove otherwise, and you would be absolved of any offense."

"Maybe so. But if I do that and you get caught, I will always blame myself for not doing everything in my power to help you. Everything! I love you, Neal. I *have to* help. Don't deny me that right!"

Neal knew that would be her response, and he knew that the will of a woman in love is beyond man's ability to restrain. But maybe he could guide her. She was very intelligent and objective. Maybe she could help without leaving any trail.

"Okay, you're right. But promise me this: you'll help me from here. Not running with me, not hiding with me, but from here, from home."

"I'm listening."

"We're both intelligent people; surely we can develop a plan. The chance of anyone in the Houston area knowing me is extremely low, and no one knows my real name."

"Well, they don't know your alias." Neal looked at her, puzzled. "Your name and photo were in the newspaper."

Neal stood to his feet, "What?"

"Your real name and picture were in the Houston Post. But you're using an alias that they don't know, and I don't think you have to worry about the picture; it was horribly unclear. It looked like they took a picture of an old picture, a Navy picture, and you were clean-shaven and had hardly any hair."

"Great! Now what?" Neal walked to the office door and leaned against the door frame. Katherine steps behind him, wraps her arms around his waist, and places her cheek against his back.

"Don't worry, Neal. We'll figure it out."

Neal stood for a moment without speaking, then turned around and held her close. He didn't want to let her go, but he knew it was time. "It's dark out. You need to get back to the house before you're missed."

"I know," she said. She leaned back and placed both hands on his cheeks. "Sleep on it. Maybe a good night's rest will help."

He chuckled, "Dreamer!"

"You hush!" she teased as she swatted his shoulder. They laughed, then she cuddled him again. "Here's what you do," she said as she stared into his eyes. "You get some sleep and leave this up to me. A woman has her ways!"

"I won't argue with that!"

"Wouldn't do you any good if you did!"

They both laughed, still holding each other close. Neal hated to let her go, but he knew she needed to get back to the house. Reluctant, he leaned over and kissed her, a gentle but firm kiss. He walked her to the door and whispered, "See you tomorrow."

"Absolutely!" she whispered back. After another quick kiss, she left him in the dark.

Neal peered out the window and watched as she skipped toward the house. He felt as if his heart danced with her. Spending time with her always made him feel that way, and when she left, she always left him with a tender heart and a hopeful spirit. With a warm smile, he watched her cross the yard and approach the house. All at once, a cold chill gripped his body! In a window on the second floor, Neal saw her father watching her every move!

The senator left his position at the window as soon as Katherine entered the house. Neal knew there was about to be a confrontation, one that wouldn't end well for either Katherine or him. Her father was an intelligent man, smart enough to suspect that Katherine's interest in the storehouse wasn't just an old family heirloom or organizing boxes. He would assume, and correctly so, that Katherine was hiding a certain petty officer that she was fond of, one who had the Navy master at arms hot on his heels!

Neal knew he couldn't leave the storeroom with any evidence of his presence. He stripped the sheets from the mattress, hid them in a box, and then placed the box in the middle of a nearby stack. The mattress itself he leaned against another stack and placed a few boxes and random items in front of it. Most of the food Benjamin brought he had eaten, except for some of the bread. He wrapped the remainder of that in a piece of paper he found on the desk, then stuffed it in his pocket. He had finished the jar of sweet tea, so he took the lid off, threw it behind some boxes, and placed the open jar on a shelf nailed to the back wall. What little trash there was, he wadded together and shoved into another pocket.

He scanned the room for any other telltale signs. It appeared he had done a good job of it, except for the jar of water. He snatched it up and rushed to the back window, opened it, and climbed outside. Careful not to make any noise, he eased the window back down then slipped over to the fence. "Another night in the forest!" he whispered. Rather than chance being seen near the back gate, Neal leaped over the fence behind the storeroom and disappeared into the darkness.

Her father met her when she entered the house. "Katherine, what exactly is your interest in the storehouse at this late hour?"

"The storehouse? W—what do you mean, Father? It's not

that late."

"I mean, why were you in the storehouse after dark? I saw you from my chamber window."

"No one calls them chambers anymore, Father. They call them bedrooms."

"Quit stalling! Is *he* hiding out there? Are you helping him?"

"I—I was just trying to—find something."

"You mean someone!" Senator Bailey stormed past her and out the side door.

Katherine spun around and followed him out. Grabbing his arm, she pleaded, "Father, please! Listen to me!"

The senator jerked his arm from her grasp but never broke stride. "If I listen to you, we'll both be doing hard time!" He stormed across the yard to the storehouse, with Katherine close on his heels. He pushed open the door and stormed in.

The storeroom was quiet and dark, lit only by a partial moon and the ambient light from the house. Scanning the room, he could see no one or even anything out of the ordinary. It all looked quite normal. His senses on edge, he crept from the front room to the office door, alert to any possible ambush or quick escape if Neal was indeed hiding there.

Katherine was petrified, afraid her father would uncover Neal at any moment. Or at least find that he'd been there and that she had helped him hide. *Poor Benjamin!* she thought. *Father would know he had helped with the mattress; it's too heavy and bulky for me. But surely, he would know that Benjamin had done only what I'd told him to do. He was ever so loyal, and Father couldn't blame him for that!*

Senator Bailey walked over to the office and stopped in the doorway to look around. Katherine was anxious as she peered around his shoulder, fearing what he would find. But she was astonished at what she saw. The mattress was gone! There was no sign of food or drink. Not even any trash lying anywhere. Her father started moving some of the boxes, looking for any hiding spot Neal might have fashioned. He moved the boxes in front of the mattress, then pulled it to the side. Behind it, there was nothing but a couple of boxes. He stood and looked around, but there was no sign of any recent activity. Even the window was closed.

Katherine was ecstatic but confused. How had Neal known her father was on to him or was coming to ransack the storeroom? Under the circumstances, how had he had the time, or presence of mind, to stash everything away? She was dumbfounded, but she knew she couldn't let her father see that.

"Satisfied, Father?"

"No!" He paused, putting his hands on his hips, appearing somewhat defeated. "Okay, so what were you doing out here?"

"Maybe, I was looking for Mother's wedding dress," she teased. "You never know; I might need it soon."

"Katherine!"

"Well, you never know! After all, I do have several suitors!" She knew her point had been understood. She would follow her own path, and her father could do nothing to change that.

"Yes, well, none that you would give the time of day." The senator stood at the open door of the storeroom, allowing her to exit first as any real southern gentleman would. Then he secured the door behind them. As they walked toward the house, he placed his arm around her shoulders and, in a low voice, advised, "Be careful, young lady!"

She smiled to herself and cupped her hand over his where it lay on her shoulder, patting it gently to let him know she understood. He had just conceded. She would have no more trouble from her father.

Chapter 12: West End Park

Daylight crept in as silent as a thief. Neal might have slept right through the morning if the clamor of the birds hadn't interrupted his dreams. Tired of sleeping in the woods, he found a quiet spot on the elevated catwalk of a railroad water caldron. The cool night breeze and the hard plank catwalk had sapped the pliability out of his muscles. He struggled to sit up. Shaking his head, he whispered, "Definitely not the Hotel Chamberlin." But at least he escaped the bugs and dampness of the forest floor.

The moist morning air began to dry out as the sun rose over the treetops. Neal rubbed his arms as the sun began to warm him, unkinking his muscles and his mind. The heat reflecting off the caldron felt inviting, but he knew he had to climb down sooner or later. It wasn't a long climb, but on the open ladder, there was nothing to hide behind. He scanned the area below for any chance observers. The only people stirring were few and far between and far enough away that the chance of being seen was remote. Being recognized from this distance, he concluded, was impossible.

When he reached the ground, he began to walk. There was no destination, but he had to move. Walking always helped clear his thoughts. His concern for Katherine had kept slumber at bay until well after midnight and was the first thing to greet his mind this morning. He had no doubt that she was a strong woman; she could handle her father. And her father would protect her from the authorities. But if he was angered enough, what measure of retaliation would he use against Neal? Katherine had sworn that her father was a reasonable man and one who would stand up for what was right. But a man will go to extreme lengths if he perceives someone to be a threat to his child, even if that threat is not physical, but one that would be a detriment to character, morals, or social reputation. And social reputation, to a man of his position, was politically critical.

"Okay, Katherine is a strong woman," he told himself. "She can handle her situation. Just think, Neal, think! You're still in a heap of trouble!" He wandered aimlessly in thought, with no destination and no cognizance of time. Soon he decided he had to let his mind rest, be void of thought and just be in the moment. *Just enjoy the morning*, he thought. It occurred to him that he still had some bread in his pocket. He pulled it out, unwrapped it, and savored the small breakfast. It wasn't much, but it was something.

He strolled along the street, enjoying the bread and taking in the sights around him. It was a nice area, not like the senator's neighborhood, but one like he'd want to live in one day. Modest homes, shops close-by, a deli and coffee shop, all very quaint and pleasant. Out of nowhere, he heard a faint sound—it was a distant but somehow familiar *crack!* He stopped in his tracks, straining to hear it again. Four or five seconds passed before he heard it again. *Crack!*

"Baseball!" he told himself. "Someone is hitting a baseball!" He followed the sound for a couple of blocks and around a corner. There in front of him was West End Park, home field for the Houston Buffalos baseball organization. It was a magnificent park, grander than anything he had seen in Louisiana, Mississippi, or Arkansas. It was even more impressive than any of the other Texas parks where he had played.

He approached the field and saw some players taking batting practice. A few of them were at or near the plate, one was pitching, and a couple were in the field chasing down the balls. There weren't enough of them to be the whole team. He decided that they were just getting a little extra practice or maybe working out some bad habits.

Standing at the fence, he watched the action, wishing he could be out there scooping up skimmers, chasing down flies, hitting his mark on throws back to the infield. After a few minutes, he worked his way up to a seat in the stands just behind the dugout. From here, he could see the whole field, from home plate to the center-field wall, without any obstruction from the fence, backstop, or grandstand structures. It was a beautiful sight! He hadn't realized how much he missed it.

Neal watched the players at all positions with an experienced and analytical eye. Soon he knew their strengths, weaknesses, style, and commitment levels. He was impressed at their level of skill, but more so that they were here working on their game outside of formal practice. That showed character. Neal liked men of character.

The batter at the plate had the strongest swing so far. Several of his hits went almost to the fence, and a couple had bounced off it. Neal watched the next pitch sail right down the middle, and the batter swung with all his might. He hit the pitch on the nose, sending a line drive scorching toward the gap in short right-center field. Both fielders charged the ball at a full run, neither watching the approach of the other. It was a brutal collision, and both players collapsed on the ground.

Neal stood and watched as the other players raced out to attend to their teammates. One of the batters ran into the stands and out a breezeway. Neal hoped he was going for help. Looking back to the field, he saw one of the injured players begin to stir and then sit up; the other had yet to move. Neal knew he had to do something. He wasn't a doctor, but he had assisted one for a while under very tough conditions at sea. He could at least assess the men to see what needed to be done.

He jumped out of the stands and ran across the field to where the men were. The one who had been sitting up was now standing with the help of the other players. The man still on the ground was conscious but was wincing in pain.

Neal looked him over. "Sir, you're okay. You're okay," Neal reassured him.

"I don't feel okay!" he growled.

"Let me check you out. Relax, lie as still as you can." Neal began to examine him. It was obvious he had a compound fracture of the right forearm, so Neal began checking other areas, finding nothing that wouldn't heal on its own if given enough time. "What's your name?"

"Bud. Bud Lynn."

"Well, Bud, you have a broken right arm, dislocated right shoulder, and some severely bruised ribs. Maybe a couple that are cracked."

"Great," Lynn replied sarcastically.

"You'll need a doctor to set the arm, but the shoulder and ribs will heal on their own in a few weeks. Bear with me for a minute, and I'll put your shoulder back in place. It might hurt a bit."

Bud held his breath as Neal reset the shoulder. He winced but never uttered a sound. Little did Neal know that the team doctor had arrived just in time to see him relocate the shoulder.

"That should do it. And you didn't even scream like a girl," Neal teased. Everyone but Bud laughed.

"Yeah, well, it hurt like Hades!" Bud paused, then added, "Thanks anyway."

"Nice job, young man," Doc commended. "You must have done that before."

Rising from his crouched position, Neal turned to see the doctor. "Yes, I have. But I left the fun work for you." Neal smiled.

Doc stooped down to examine Bud's arm. "Ah, the boy will be fine. But he *will* scream like a girl when I reset that bone." Again, Bud was the only one who didn't find anything humorous, not anything at all. "Bud, you think you can stand up?"

"I think so, doc." In a few short minutes, they had Bud up and into the doc's motorcar, along with the other less-injured fielder. Within seconds they were on their way to the clinic. The rest of the players returned to the infield.

"Good work, man. Thanks!" the pitcher said, extending his hand to Neal. "I'm Coach Hill, the team manager."

Neal shook his hand. "I'm Nea—James. James Landis."

119

"Nice to meet you, James." The other players introduced themselves in turn, all thankful for Neal's quick attentiveness to Bud's injuries.

Coach Hill said, "Okay, we need to go ahead and finish batting practice. We're a little short-handed, but we'll just have to make do. One in the box, one in the hole, the rest of you on the field." The players turned to take their places.

"Coach Hill?" Neal said.

"Yes, sir?"

"I used to play a lot, not that long ago. I'd be glad, be honored, to help in the field."

Coach Hill paused for a moment, then yelled, "Charlie! Give James a glove."

"Thank you, coach," Neal replied.

Charlie pitched a glove at Neal. He deftly caught the glove in mid-air with one hand, nodded at Charlie, then trotted out to center field. He feigned total calmness and nonchalance, but inside he was ecstatic! After all the predicaments he'd found himself in over the last several weeks, who could've imagined he'd be standing in a Texas League ballfield taking practice with the Houston Buffalos team! Neal chuckled. *This is so bizarre*, he told himself.

Neal placed the glove on his left hand and smacked it in the palm several times with his right fist. How natural it felt like it was an extension of his flesh. He raised his gloved hand to his nose, smelled the leather, and chewed the end of the thong that secured the webbing. Wafting through the warm morning air was the clean, sweet aroma of fresh cut grass. The voices of the players echoed from the grandstands, bouncing around the field several times before fading below discernable decibel levels.

Neal felt the stress leave his body. He became totally relaxed. The field felt like home—like this is what he was born to do. He was at peace, true peace. This was the most at peace he had been since right after his last ballgame in Ruston and his conversation with Veldon Maxwell, Scout for the Shreveport Pirates. It seemed like forever ago, in another life.

"You better warm up." Neal's thoughts were jerked back into the present. He turned just in time to catch a throw from Charlie, who had jogged out onto the field behind him. It was a snap reaction, but he caught the ball squarely in the pocket of the glove. He gripped the ball with his right hand and squeezed it, observing the ever-so-slight way the rubber core submitted to pressure. Turning it in his fingers, he relished the old familiar feel of the smooth horse-leather cover. Then he placed his two forefingers across the seams and tossed the ball back to Charlie. It felt good, though he could tell he hadn't thrown in a while. But it didn't take long to warm up, and soon his throws were landing in Charlie's glove with a loud *whap!*

From the infield, he heard Coach Hill yell, "Batter up!"

He and Charlie took positions on either side of center field, Neal toward the left-field side, Charlie toward the right. A couple of players took the short field positions, and two others took infield spots. Neal planted his feet in the ankle-high grass and took the ready position.

The first two hits were long, lazy flies to Charlie. Neal watched as Charlie caught the flies and threw the ball to the cutoff man near second base, making it look easy. The next hit was a two-hopper to Neal. He scooped it up and, like Charlie did, threw it to the cutoff man. The next several hits were grounders or easy pop flies scattered back and forth between the infield and outfield.

The next batter was a right-hander with power. Neal shifted over to left field, and Charlie hung out just right of dead center. The first couple of hits were hot grounders down the third baseline. Neal picked them up and threw them to the cutoff man. The next was a line drive to center field. Neal watched as Charlie made an easy play of it, catching it chest high at a moderate run and side arming the ball back to the cutoff.

The next pitch was met with the full power of the batter. It was a screaming fly ball to deep left-center. Neal took off like a bullet. It was a long run from where he started, but his speed was second to none back in Louisiana. As the ball dropped just short of the fence, Neal made a dive for it, catching the spinning sphere just inches above the ground.

"Holy smokes, what a catch!" Charlie shouted. The other players on the field were all cheering and yelling compliments to Neal. Except for Coach Hill. He had seen a lot of lucky catches, and he wasn't sure this wasn't just another one.

"Keep hitting them to the left side," he told the batter. "Work him."

The batter smiled; he knew what the coach was thinking. As Neal trotted back toward his previous position, Coach Hill waved to Charlie to move over to right field. Charlie grinned, then slid over to the right.

Crack! A line drive over the shortstop. Neal charged at an angle and caught the ball knee-high at a full run. Coach Hill quickly pitched before Neal could reposition himself. The hit was a pop-up, high over third base. Neal got to it so fast he had to wait for it to come down. The test continued for the next two batters. Neal never missed a catch.

Then Pat, the last batter, stepped up to bat. "Home plate!" Coach Hill shouted out to the fielders. Charlie got the first hit, a one hopper in short right center. He picked it up and let it fly, reaching home plate in the air. The next hit was to Neal, a short two-hopper. Neal scooped it up and, since it was a somewhat short throw, made a moderate toss to home plate.

"This isn't toss and catch!" Coach Hill shouted. "Throw it!"

The next hit was straight at Neal in the middle of left field. Neal played it a little deep, and as the fly ball descended earthward, he charged in for the catch. In one swift move, he caught the ball and launched it to home plate. It hissed as it cut through the air, never getting over ten feet off the ground, and crossed home plate a perfect strike.

"Nice!" yelled Charlie.

Coach Hill was impressed but wasn't convinced. "Hit it over there again, Pat."

"Gladly, coach. That's my strong side!"

Several more hits flew into left field, and each time Neal sent the ball scorching back to home, hitting his target every time. Coach Hill was impressed. "One more," he told Pat.

This one was a blast, flying deep into left field. Neal turned and ran straight for the outfield wall. It was well over his head, but he was determined to reach it and committed to the catch. It was an all-out race with no chance for thinking or timing. As the ball sailed over his head, Neal dove with all his strength, stretching as far as he could to intercept the trajectory of the dropping ball. Straining to reach, sailing through the air, never taking his eyes off the ball, he watched as it fell into his glove and stuck between his thumb and index finger in the edge of the webbing, half in his glove, half out.

Neal hit the ground and rolled, bounced onto his feet, and with one quick step, sent the ball hissing toward home plate. It was a perfectly aligned one-hopper to the catcher.

"Woohoo, yeah!" Charlie shouted. "That's it, James!"

The name startled Neal. He had been so engrossed in his performance that, for a moment, he had forgotten he told them to call him James. "Thanks!" he replied.

The other players jumped and cheered, showing their amazement at the play. Coach Hill smiled and gazed across the field at Neal. Shaking his head, he muttered, "Incredible!" He waved for Neal and Charlie to come in from the field. As Neal crossed the infield, the players shook his hand and patted him on the back, complimenting his play in left field. Coach Hill's expression was solemn as Neal approached him. "Nice job, James," coach said.

"Thank you."

"I just have one question." Neal glanced up, waiting. Coach proffered a bat to Neal and said, "Can you hit?"

Neal smiled and responded, "Generally."

"Yes, well, show me what 'generally' looks like." The players laughed, and a couple slapped Neal on the back for encouragement. "Ned, you pitch. Charlie, catch. The rest of you get in the field." They hustled to their positions in anticipation of what this new man could do. If his batting was anything close to his fielding, he just might be one of the best players any of them had ever seen.

Ned took his place on the mound, and Neal took his at the plate. Coach Hill instructed Neal to bunt five, then meet five. No hard swings; just hit the ball on the nose. Neal did as he was instructed without flaw.

"Okay," Coach said, "hit away."

Neal scraped some dirt away with his right heel to make a comfortable place to plant his back foot. He didn't have cleats, so batting with street shoes required a solid foothold so his slick soles wouldn't slip.

The first couple of hits were solid, hard ground balls. Neal liked the feel of the bat as there was almost no rebound. But then, Ned wasn't throwing all that hard either. The next few hits were hard and placed expertly—right field, center field, left field. Then he reversed it—left field, center field, right field. Coach Hill was pleased with Neal's ability to place the ball. It showed his control of the bat and ability to hit for the gaps when the conditions required it.

Neal stepped out of the batter's box and turned to Coach Hill. "Can he throw any faster than that?"

Coach Hill laughed. "Bring 'em in, Ned! Full speed!"

Ned took his full windup then shot a blazing fastball right down the middle. Neal was ready, and his timing was perfect. The bat met the ball with a loud *crack*, and the report of the hit echoed all around the stadium. The ball lifted into the air as if on wings, sailing way over the head of the fielders. They could do nothing but watch as the sphere continued its path until landing out of sight beyond the center field wall.

At first, no one spoke. Out-of-the-park home runs happened but were rare. The rubber-centered baseballs of the day just didn't fly that well. All eyes turned to Neal in amazement. He was pleased with the hit, but the silence made him uncomfortable.

"Luck, maybe?" he said.

"I doubt it," Coach Hill chuckled. "That kind of power isn't luck." Then he turned to the mound, "Give 'em all you' got, Ned!"

Over the next few minutes, Neal had the outfielders backed up to the wall. Hit after hit showed sheer power, some in the air and some on the ground. Several bounced off the wall, but just two more cleared the wall.

Coach Hill yelled, "All in!" Then he walked over and put his arm around Neal's shoulder and led him to a place near the dugout. "Okay, James, I'm a believer—you can play, as good as any I've seen. But tell me, what kind of league experience do you have?"

"Well," Neal said, almost as if ashamed to say. "Most recently, I played independent league in Louisiana. We played teams from other cities and towns, and occasionally teams from other states in open tournaments."

"Did you ever have any scouts talk to you?"

"Yes, sir, I did. But I had my heart set on going into—I mean, I wanted to travel. My dad is a surveyor, and I thought I would take a short break to travel some and then come back and work with him."

"I understand. But let me tell you, son, a talent like yours doesn't come around too often. You could make a name in this business." Neal just nodded. "I tell you what…you know we're short on players, and I really could use some help."

"Yes, sir."

"There's only one game left in the season, and if your name is on the roster for that game, you qualify to play in the playoffs." Coach paused for a moment to let the info sink in. "How about it?"

Neal hesitated; his thoughts were tangled in knots. "I don't know."

"What's the problem? It's easy to see you love the game, and I *need* your help!"

"Well, I'm staying with a friend right now and really don't want to impose for an extended period."

"That's not an issue. You can stay here!"

"Are you sure?"

"Absolutely! You can sleep anywhere you want. There are showers and toilets in the dressing room, and there are plenty of places to eat close by. You can even bring your friend over here any time you want. You'll have the run of the place. What do you say?"

"Well, I'd love to, but—"

"Did I mention you get paid?"

Neal laughed, "That always helps!"

"Yeah, I thought it might!"

"Ha! Okay, I tell you what," Neal wipes the sweat from his face. "Let me talk with my friend about it, and I'll give you an answer tomorrow."

"Deal!" Coach Hill shakes Neal's hand, and the other players cheer in approval. As Neal walks toward the fence gate, Coach yells, "James!" Neal turns to face him. "Practice at 8 a.m." He smiles and nods, then exits through the gate.

Chapter 13: The Risk

His mind was racing as he made his way back to Katherine's house. How strange a turn of events this was! And what an opportunity! He was ecstatic at the chance to play and to get paid for something he loved! But at the same time, was this too much of a risk—to put himself on display in front of hundreds, possibly thousands of people? Maybe. Maybe not. Yes, Texas is a neighboring state to Louisiana, but Houston is hundreds of miles from Bienville. Chances were, no one would know him. If anyone he knew *did* come to Houston, the best way would be to ride on the train, and the depot is quite a distance from West End Park. The chance of being seen by anyone who knew him would be less than his chance of walking on the moon.

Neal made it to Katherine's house in record time. He passed through the back gate, then slipped along the fence line through the woods to the back of the storage building. There, he stood for a while, listening for any sounds coming from inside. There was nothing but silence. He inched over to peek through the window but saw no one. Inserting his fingertips as much as possible under the bottom window rail, he tried to open the back window; it wouldn't budge. He stood on his toes and peered through the glass to check the latch; it was locked!

With palms on either side of the window, he leaned over and rested his weight against the wall. Head down and eyes closed in exasperation, he took a deep breath, exhaled slowly, then whispered to himself, "Now what?" The only other way to get into the building was the front door if it was unlocked, and he couldn't try that until after dark. All he could do was lay low in the bushes and wait.

He eased away from the storehouse and into the woods to a patch of shrubs along the fence line. From this vantage point, he watched the storage building for activity and had a couple of sightlines to the yard beyond; one to the front yard, one to the back. It was a good spot to hide. The brush was so thick a bloodhound would have a hard time finding him, yet his field of view was good as long as it was daylight.

He waited. And waited. It seemed like forever, an eternity of nothingness except for the occasional bird flitting through the low branches, trying to find its last meal before settling in to roost. Dusk was beginning to fade to darkness. Neal knew it wouldn't be long before he could make his move to the front door. He was rising to work his way to the back of the storage building when he heard an automobile approaching.

It appeared in the driveway at the front of the house and came to a stop at the foot of the entryway steps. It was Benjamin in the Ford Model K, with Katherine and Senator Bailey in the back seat. Katherine was seated behind Benjamin, her father on the passenger side. Neal crouched behind the bushes, watching in earnest, striving to calculate his next move. Somehow, he had to let Katherine know he was here.

The senator got out first. His feet had just touched the ground when Benjamin arrived to assist Katherine out of the car. From his position, Neal could only see the ends of the first couple of steps peeking around the corner of the house. The senator rushed up the stairway and passed out of sight.

Benjamin closed the car door then followed Katherine around to the front of the Ford. Neal left his hiding spot in the shrubs and made his way to the back corner of the storage building, hoping to get the chance to catch Katherine's attention. As she started up the steps, he took a step out from behind the building and released a short, quick whistle, "♫!"

Benjamin caught the sound and glanced over to see Neal standing in the shadow of the woods. Katherine continued up the steps. "Miss Katherine, I'm gonna put da motor carriage unner da shed."

"Thank you, Benjamin."

"And Miss Katherine, affer you go inside an' 'scuse yourself to your room, y—you might wanna take a little after-dark stroll." He glanced over and nodded toward the storage building. "It calms da nerves after a worrisome day."

She shot a gaze to the storage building for a moment, then looked back at him. At once, Katherine's eyes flew open wide! With a pleasant and grateful smile, she replied, "Thank you, Benjamin! That sounds like a good idea." She walked into the house and closed the door behind her.

Benjamin turned toward Neal and, using hand gestures, directed him to go into the storage building. He then started up the Ford and drove it to the shed. Neal crept to the front door of the building; it was unlocked. He opened the door just enough to slip inside, then closed it back. He leaned his back against the door and took a deep breath. For a while, he just stood in the darkness, glad to be back in a familiar place.

Katherine would be coming, soon he hoped. But until then, he needed rest.

After his eyes had time to adjust, he moved to the back room and found the mattress exactly as he had stashed it. He moved the boxes from in front of it and placed them against the wall. He set up the blocks and planks and placed the mattress on them as Benjamin had done on the first night. He sat on the edge of the mattress for a while, then stretched out to unwind.

So much had happened today. He couldn't wait to tell Katherine the news! She would be thrilled for him! This is what he always wanted to do. He would explain to her how it all had happened, every step that led him to the field, how the player had been injured and how he offered to fill in for the practice session. How he had played the field and hit the ball, and how Coach Hill made him the offer, with pay! He knew she would be happy for him, maybe concerned too, but happy. He would tell her he'd thought about the negatives, but they were few and very unlikely to occur. Maybe she would agree that the familiar activity, which he loved so much, would help relieve his stress, give him clarity of mind. And maybe his subconscious would help him develop a plan to prove his innocence to the officials. Maybe. At the least, he could have a few hours escape from the hovering shadow of his situation.

Then the doorknob turned! Neal froze in place; he'd been so wrapped up in his thoughts that he hadn't been watching for visitors, wanted or otherwise. The door began to open. There was no place to hide and no time to get there if he found one. All he could do was lie still, motionless. His only hope was that whoever it was would stay in the front room or that it was Katherine.

He heard footsteps fall on the wooden floor as the faint light from the open door pierced the darkness of the room. "Neal? Neal, are you here?"

The grip of fear released him as he recognized Katherine's small, quiet voice. He blew out the deep breath he didn't realize he was holding. Rising from the bed, he replied, "Yes, I'm here." He met her in the front room, wrapped his arms around her, and held her close. "I've missed you!"

She squeezed him to her breast. "And I've missed you!" She rose to her toes and kissed him, then looked up at him in alarm. "I was so afraid Father was going to catch you last night!"

"He almost did! I think he was coming in the front door when I was closing the back window. It was close!"

"I was so scared!" Katherine released him, and with a puzzled look, asked, "How did you know—"

"When you walked back to the house last night, I saw your father watching you from the upstairs window."

"Thank goodness! I don't see how you had time to hide everything—the mattress and planks, the food, wraps, and sweet tea containers!"

"Ha! Stuffed the bread in my pocket!"

"No, you didn't!"

"It tasted great this morning!" he teased.

She laughed. "You're hopeless!"

"Well, it's all I had. In fact, that's all I've had all day."

"I can remedy that. There is plenty of food in the kitchen," she replied. "But seriously, I've been worried about you. Where did you go last night? And where have you been today?"

"I slept on the catwalk of a water caldron. I think it was about a mile from here. Anyway, let me tell you about today!"

"Oh, me! You sound rather excited. Did you make a breakthrough on your case?"

"Well, no, not really. But I got a great opportunity, at least for a little while!"

"That's great! Tell me!"

"Okay. After I climbed down from the caldron, I started walking just to clear my head. I was worried for you, you know, afraid your father would make things hard for you because of me."

"I can handle Father."

"Yes, I'm quite certain of that. But I just don't want you to have to 'handle' anything. Anyway, I was walking trying to figure things out, and then I heard a noise like a 'crack.'"

"Crack?"

"Yes. Then another 'crack,' and I thought, baseball, somebody's playing baseball! So, I followed the sound until I reached this big stadium with huge bleachers and everything. It was the Houston Buffalos! The Houston Buffalos baseball team, at least some of them. They were practicing. You know I love baseball! So, I watched for a little while, and it helped me get my mind off things, off my situation."

"Good." Katherine was amused by Neal's growing

excitement.

"Then you know what happened? A player got hurt!"

"Hurt?"

"Yes! These two fielders were chasing the same fly ball, and *wham!* they slammed into each other! Both of them fell out on the ground dazed and moaning."

Katherine teased, "Oh, no! Did they catch the ball?"

"That's not the point! The point is I was a medic's aid in the Navy—"

"That's the point?"

"No! Stop it!" Neal smiled; Katherine laughed. "I'm trying to tell you what happened."

"I think you're, darling!"

"The point is they got hurt, and because *darling* here was a medic's aid in the Navy, I ran out on the field to help. One of the guys was okay, but the other had a broken arm and a dislocated shoulder."

"Oh, no!"

"Yes, he really got his bell rung. So, I put the shoulder back in place. The doc said I did a great job."

"Doc? What doc? Why didn't the doc do it?"

"Because the doc wasn't there—"

"You just said he was there. You said he said you did a good job."

Neal took a deep breath, exhaled, and stared at Katherine

with his hands on his hips. Katherine laughed and put her arms around Neal's waist. "Okay, young lady," he said. "The doctor was in the locker room, and by the time someone ran to get him and bring him onto the field, I was already in the process of relocating the shoulder."

"I'm proud of you! You *have* had a good day."

"Yes, but that's still not the best part."

"Oh, well, tell me!"

"I'm trying to!" he snapped, but he couldn't help but smile. Katherine laughed and stretched up and gave him a quick kiss. Neal continued, "Both players had to leave the field, so they were short-handed. I offered to play the field, so they let me! I practiced with the Buffalos!"

"How fun!"

"Yes, but that's not all. They liked the way I played. So, they asked if I would play out the season with them! Isn't that great?"

Katherine was alarmed. "What do you mean?"

"They put me on the team! I'm going to play in the playoffs with them as an actual team member!"

"Neal! You can't be serious! You've been hiding for weeks, and now you want to put yourself on display in front of hundreds of people? It's insane!"

"No, Katherine. I've thought about it. There are only a few games left. No one in town knows me, and I seriously doubt any secret agent who's looking for me will be attending a baseball game. I mean, the odds are extremely remote."

"What about the team you played for in Louisiana or any of the other teams you played against? Will any of them be in the playoffs? They'll know you."

"We were in a different league; none of them are eligible at this level. It's okay."

"Well, I don't like it. It's much too risky."

"It'll be fine!"

"You don't know that. You have no clue who might be there!"

"Katherine, there's nothing to worry about. Nobody here knows me."

Katherine's eyes flew wide in alarm. "Neal! Dr. George has season tickets to the Buffalos' games. He knows you!"

Neal stood for a moment processing the thought. "Wait, let's not overreact. Think about it; he only met me once, six or seven months ago. I barely even talked with him; I have a beard, and my hair is longer now, so I look different."

"Neal, seven months is not a long time. We sat and talked together at the table. Of course, he'll remember you."

"Okay, we talked some. But he was distracted by a lot of other people during that time. He's a very well-known man, and I'm just some sailor. Why would he remember me?"

"Because you were there with *me*, that's why! I told you how he is with women."

"Yes, you did. But remember, that was a busy night, we talked very little, he was drinking, and I looked different. Besides, I'll be way out in the field. He won't even get a good look at me."

"What about when you're batting?"

"When I'm batting, I'll be facing the opposite direction—I hope. Look, you have nothing to worry about. Trust me!"

She paused for a moment. "I still say it's too risky…but it's probably useless to try to talk you out of it."

"You're probably right," Neal teased. He put his arms around her and pulled her close. "It'll be okay. I promise." She laid her head on his chest, and for a moment, they stood still, neither speaking. Neal broke the silence, "By the way, Coach Hill told me I could stay at the stadium. There's a bunk and a shower."

"So, you'd rather stay there than come see me?"

"Of course not! I'll see you. But staying here will soon get me caught. The senator already knows I sneak in and out, and getting food is a chore. Wait—didn't you mention something earlier about food?"

"Um—no thanks, I'm not hungry."

"Why you—!"

They began to tussle in fun, playing, giggling, and laughing, but careful not to create too much noise. Soon the intimacy of the play, proximity, and touch yielded to attraction and desire. Neal pulled her close and wrapped his arms around her waist, holding her tighter than she had ever allowed anyone to before. In the semi-darkness of the room, they gazed deep into each other's eyes. Sheltered in the quiet confines of the storage building by the woods, they kissed softly, tenderly, deeply.

Katherine had never experienced a feeling like this before, a feeling that was so deep, mysterious, and exciting. Her face flushed, her heart raced, and a wave of warmth passed from her head to her feet. She yearned for more. For the first time in her life, she understood why some lay restraint aside and yield to passion.

But Katherine had lived by a strict set of values with boundaries she would not allow herself to violate. Doing so would only complicate her life and dishonor Neal, not to mention the disappointment her father would feel. Besides, Neal hadn't even attempted anything inappropriate, and she refused to be the aggressor.

Katherine broke the silence. "I would love to just stay here and hold you forever, but I need to go back inside."

"I know," Neal replied.

They didn't move. Each just stood holding the other as if it was the last time they would ever be together. After a few minutes, Neal released her. Taking her by the hand, he led her to the door. "I'll be out early; I need to get to the field. Practice starts at 8 a.m. sharp. Oh, and I'm going to stay at the stadium tomorrow night. I don't want any unexpected visitors. You know what they say, 'creatures of habit are easy prey.'"

"Who says that?"

"Well, um, you know, *they* do."

"Mm-hmm," she smiled. Then the smile faded. "Be careful!" With that, Katherine kissed him goodnight and exited the door.

As she made her way back to the house, her concern for Neal occupied her every thought. There was always a chance that someone would recognize him at the game. She couldn't bear the thought of him being arrested, humiliated in front of hundreds of people at the game. They would find him guilty without ever giving him the chance to clear himself, guilty even if he was found innocent later by a jury.

She had to think; to devise a plan to get Neal out of the stadium should he be recognized. But how? There had to be a way. And if she got him out, where would he, they, go? She was too well known in Houston. If she left with him, they couldn't go home; that would be the first place the feds would go. It had to be an out-of-the-way place, obscure, someplace no one would suspect.

But first, she had to get him out of the stadium. That was the first obstacle. And the stadium was built like a trap. Tall grandstands stood behind the plate and extended to the bases on either side, and the field was surrounded by fencing as tall, maybe even taller, than Neal. She would tell him to go to the field and find all the exits, gates, employee doors, any path that wasn't likely to be congested when the stadium was full. They had to know in advance. That was their only chance to make it out.

Katherine was startled by a loud noise from downstairs. She jumped up and ran to the head of the staircase, where she glanced down and saw her father inspecting the front door as if looking for damage.

"Father, what on earth was that noise?"

Closing the door, he replied, "That was Dr. George testing the craftsmanship of the entry door." He gazed up at her and added, "Thankfully, I believe it passed muster."

"What happened?"

"We just had a difference of opinion, that's all. Don't worry, dear. He'll be fine once he has time to mull it over."

As Katherine descended the stairs, she said, "Father, I don't like that man. He's evil!"

"Ha! I don't know that I'd go that far, but I think his past is about to redirect his future."

"Good!" she said as she reached her father at the bottom of the staircase.

"Good?"

"Father, you know I don't wish anyone harm. But if there was ever a man that needed redirecting, it would definitely be Dr. George."

Senator Bailey placed his hands on her shoulders, searing her with a suspicious gaze typical of a protective father. "What has he done, Katherine? Has he ever overstepped his bounds with you?"

"He's made plenty of attempts, but I quickly put him in his place! Don't you worry about me!" He relaxed his grip on her. Katherine continued, "But the poor girls in his office have no choice but to put up with him or quit!"

Senator Bailey put his arm around her shoulder as she began moving toward the kitchen. "He does have a lot of employee turnover. Have any of them ever talked to you about what— what it's like to work for him?"

"Yes. And what goes on there, too. It's awful!"

"Can you tell me about it?"

She paused for a moment. "Can we discuss it later? I'm

starved right now, and talking about it may cause me to lose my appetite."

The senator laughed. "That bad, is it?" Katherine didn't respond. "Okay, later will be fine," he said. "I think I could use a snack myself."

After cheese, crackers, milk, and small talk, she bid her father goodnight and retired to her room. It wasn't late but worry exhausted her. She sat at her dresser and began to take down her hair. The familiar surroundings caused her mind to return to her earlier thoughts of Neal.

"I have to tell Neal to find the exits," she reminded herself. Realizing she couldn't leave the house again for fear of arousing Father's suspicions, a thought occurred to her. *Benjamin! I must get Benjamin to go tell him!* She made a quick check of her hair in the mirror. It fell in soft waves over her shoulders, but the bangs were still pinned and presentable. "That's just like a woman," her father would say, "vanity before calamity!" The thought that he knew her so well somewhat disturbed her, but that just served to focus her efforts. She tiptoed to the door and listened for a moment; nothing. She turned the doorknob and moved the door just enough to peek out through a sliver of an opening. Again, nothing. Then she opened it wide enough to slide through, and, without a sound, she closed it behind her.

Descending the stairs, she heard her father stirring in the study. She could smell the tobacco from his pipe, a rich smell accented by the sweetness of the sliced apples he always added for flavor. She had loved that smell since childhood. More than once, she had located her father by following the aroma of the apples. But this was a time to avoid him. She slipped past the study and continued through the hall and into the kitchen.

The senator's house had electrical service, a luxury that the wealthier neighborhoods of Houston had enjoyed for years. Most of the housemaids and yardmen had never seen electrical lights other than a few streetlights scattered throughout parts of Houston. When Benjamin was hired to be the family carriage driver, he was single; his wife had passed the previous year from a hard spell of pneumonia. He had no family near, so the senator moved him into an outbuilding on the east side of the property. Benjamin called it the cottage. Katherine thought her father was quite ingenious when he decided to stretch wires across the yard to the cottage. In the house, the ends of the wires were attached to a switch in the kitchen. The other ends were attached to a light in Benjamin's cottage. When a family member or the housemaid needed him, they would flip the switch to turn on the light. Posthaste Benjamin would be standing at the back door.

Katherine stepped across the kitchen to the switch and, with intense care, eased it to the "on" position. She tiptoed into the pantry and opened the window, waiting for him to approach. As he neared the house, Katherine called in a loud whisper, "Benjamin! Benjamin! Over here!" He saw her standing at the window and made his way to her.

"Benjamin, you must do me a favor. Go to the storage building and tell Neal to count the exits in the stadium tomorrow."

"Exits?"

"Yes! Every door, gate, or hole in the fence. Tell him to find them and memorize where they are."

"Yes, Miss Katherine. I'll sure do dat. Do—do I need to

give him a reason, ma'am?"

"He'll know. Just tell him."

"Yes, ma'am, I'll do dat right now."

Katherine watched as Benjamin headed toward the storehouse. "Good! That's done," she told herself. Now she had the task of getting back to her room without alerting her father. She slipped through the kitchen and up the hall, then began to tiptoe up the stairs as quietly as possible. About halfway up the staircase, she heard the familiar click of the study doorknob as her father opened the door. She spun around and started back down the stairs as her father stepped out of the study.

"Katherine! I thought you would be asleep by now."

"I should be father, but I have a bit of a dry mouth. I'm going to the kitchen for a glass of water."

"I see," he said as he met her at the bottom of the staircase. "Turn the stair light off when you come back through."

She gave him a sly smile as she paused to look him in the eye. "I will, Father. I always do." She gave him a quick peck on the cheek and sauntered toward the kitchen. Her father ascended the stairs and retired to his bedroom.

Katherine let out a sigh of relief. *That was close!* she told herself. *But it might not be over, as Father may decide to come back out of his room for some reason.* In a wise move, she decided to proceed to the kitchen to complete the façade. She took a glass from the cupboard, filled it from the tap, and made her way back to her bedroom.

Back in her room, her mind raced with thought as she

dressed for bed. At first, she took the position of an attorney, trying to build a rational case for Neal's acquittal. But there was no alibi and no witness to verify his innocence other than the two fugitives, who would be crazy not to try to cast the blame on him to clear themselves. Then she would take the path of the escape artist, which, she determined, would be easier once Neal found all the exits from the stadium. But even if they got out, where would they go? To whom could they turn for help and asylum? Money was not an issue; she had plenty to last a year or more. The problem was how to get it from the bank without being detained...unless she withdrew her funds before the escape. But then, her father was friends with the banker, and if she closed her account, he would surely contact the senator about it before she and Neal had a chance to get away.

"What other options are there?" she asked herself aloud. "I wish Father had some dirt on a judge!" But knowing her father's character, she admitted, "He wouldn't use it to help Neal. Daddy's too stinking ethical! And loyal." Feeling defeated, depressed, and very exhausted, she turned down the sheets and got into bed. *I'm too tired to think about it anymore*, she told herself. *I need sleep. Maybe sleep will help clear my mind.*

The night had been anything but restful for Katherine. She was certain of Neal's innocence and obsessed with his escape. But try as she might, every plan she concocted was overshadowed by the same basic questions: how would they escape, where would they go, how would they get there, what would they do after they got there, what happens when her money is spent, do they get jobs, what happens if they're recognized, what if the authorities catch up to them, will the cycle start over again, will it ever end? At last, she dozed off sometime before dawn.

She woke to the embrace of her heavy quilt and the smell of bacon, her favorite breakfast aroma. Estimating her night's sleep at about three hours, she decided to go ahead and get out of bed as the night probably had given her all the sleep she was going to get. Besides, by the time she donned her house dress and brushed her hair, the eggs and biscuits would no doubt be ready to eat.

Katherine reached the bottom of the stairs and noticed the library doors closed. Apparently, her father had eaten early and retired to his library, no doubt absorbed in some new legislative endeavor or a good fiction read. He enjoyed tales about the common man, especially those told by authors such as Tolstoy, Dickens, and George Eliot. In reality, Eliot was a woman. But that had never been an issue to her father; he was quite novel in his respect for women. His favorite writer was Mark Twain, whom the senator had met and had conversations with on several occasions. Their connection was immediate, as their demeanors were similar—even-tempered and composed. And their strengths were oddly complementary; her father's were compassion and vision, Twain's were humor and vision. Katherine always thought they would have made a great team. So as not to disturb him, she sneaked past the library and on toward the bacon.

Chapter 14: Veldon Maxwell

Veldon Maxwell put his tote bag and plenty of fuel in his 1906 Pierce Racine Model D, an automobile the Shreveport Pirates provided to him for use on team business. It wasn't a glamorous vehicle, but it was practical. It came complete with enough horsepower to handle rough roads and the occasional steep incline and included a windshield and covered seating to facilitate operation in inclement weather. Mr. Maxwell enjoyed traveling, and the Model D made his scouting trips a pleasure.

After a full day of meetings, paperwork, and some domestic tasks at home, he left Shreveport in the late afternoon, hoping to reach Bienville by dark. The roads on his route were dirt or gravel and were apt to be bad in spots. But rain had been scarce for weeks, so he was optimistic about his ability to make good time.

Dusk was almost gone when he arrived in Bienville, a bit later than he had hoped. He was right about the roads; they were in decent condition. What he hadn't accounted for was the amount of traffic on the way, the four-legged kind. Most livestock in the area was not yet accustomed to the clackety-clack of automobile engines, so each interaction presented its own challenge, and most were time-consuming affairs.

He stopped to inquire as to the location of a boarding house and was directed to the only one in town. He didn't have much in the way of luggage. Just a tote bag with a change of clothes and toiletries, all he needed for a one-night stay. After parking the Pierce in the alley, he entered the establishment and booked a room for the night.

The following morning, he was back in the lobby at 7 a.m. The clerk behind the counter was busy reading The Weekly Argus, a local newspaper. He approached the clerk and asked, "Excuse me?" The clerk lowered the paper just enough to peer over the top. "Can you tell me if there is a restaurant close by?"

With a nod of his head, the clerk responded, "Poland's Café, just down the street." He resumed his reading.

"Thank you, sir!" Mr. Maxwell left the lobby and walked out to the front porch, feeling dapper in his Homburg hat, clean sack coat, and two-toned calfskin lace-up shoes. He watched as businesses began to open up, and a bit of traffic began to trickle down the main street. It was a beautiful morning, albeit a little warm. He knew that in another hour or two, the sun would be burning the dew off the trees and grass, making the air so humid it would collect on the metal rooftops and fall from the edges in a slow, monotonous drip, drip, drip.

He spotted the café just three doors down and across the street. He made the short walk, entered the café, and sat at a table pushed against the wall on the far side of the room. Dust from the dry street had covered his shoes and floated up onto his trousers. He swatted the top of his trousers with his fingertips, sending dust into the bright morning sunlight shining through the front glass of the café. The particles sparkled and flickered like fireflies as they floated lazily in and out of the rays, swirling excitedly as passersby disturbed the stagnant air. Patrons, mostly in small groups of two or three, sat scattered about.

"Water, sir?" A diminutive man with a stained apron placed a glass on the table.

"Thank you," Mr. Maxwell replied.

"Special of the day is eggs—any way you want 'em— 'taters, biscuits, and your choice of bacon, ham, or steak."

"Okay. Scrambled and bacon, crunchy."

"We have sliced tomatoes if you like and milk fresh from the jersey."

Mr. Maxwell nodded, "Yes, please. Both!" The words were barely uttered before the waiter disappeared into the kitchen.

He began to study the people around the room, noticing two or three men who appeared to be in their fifties or older. He wondered if they knew Neal. It seemed probable in a town this small that somebody would know him. Maybe, he thought, maybe one of these men could be Neal's father. But that would be unlikely. He decided not to disturb any of them during their meal, if at all. His best option was to relax and have a good breakfast, and then, when paying his bill, he would inquire as to the location of the Crowson home.

The portions were large and cooked to perfection, and Mr. Maxwell soon realized that he had devoured much more than wisdom would have suggested. He sat up to let it all settle, placed his napkin over his plate, and rested his hands in his lap.

Only a few short minutes had passed, and the waiter was

again at his table. "How was breakfast, sir?"

"Wonderful, thank you!"

"Would you like coffee?"

"No, I think I'd just like to sit for a few minutes," he said, patting his belly with both hands.

"Take your time, sir." Motioning toward a desk near the front door, he added, "When you're ready, you can pay Mr. Poland at the register." Maxwell nodded.

Over the next few minutes, Poland's Café became a bit more active as more patrons came in for their morning fare. Mr. Maxwell decided to yield his table to the new diners strolling in, an act he was sure the owner would appreciate.

As he approached the cash register, he was met with a friendly smile from a large, middle-aged man. "How was your meal?"

"Excellent! I think I'm going to need a nap," he joked.

"Good! I want everyone to leave happy and full."

"You succeeded here!" Maxwell laughed. "You are the owner?"

"Yes." Offering his hand, he introduced himself, "Tom Poland."

"Veldon Maxwell." They shook hands.

"I don't believe I've seen you in here before, Mr. Maxwell."

"No, probably not. I've only been here once before, about a year ago on business."

"Oh?"

"I'm a talent scout for the Shreveport Pirates baseball team, Texas League. I came to recruit one of your local players, Neal Crowson." He noticed a change in Poland's demeanor, not a look of distaste, but more of surprise and concern. "I plan to visit his parents today."

In a somewhat hushed tone, Poland responded, "Neal was always a good boy. Know his parents well. It's a shame he's in the mess he's in."

Maxwell was shocked. "Mess? What mess?"

"You haven't heard?"

"No, nothing! I thought he joined the Navy?"

"Maybe I shouldn't have said anything," Poland apologized. "After all, we only have bits and pieces from random out-of-town papers. We really don't know all the facts."

"Okay, what facts do you know?"

"Well, as you said, he left town to join the Navy; had high hopes of getting assigned to the Great White Fleet."

"Yes, he told me he was going to do that."

Poland continued, "Well, he made it! Was assigned to the U. S. S. Virginia. They left the Hampton Rhodes docks last December just before Christmas."

Somewhat perturbed, Mr. Maxwell interjected, "Yes, I've been following the Fleet, and I know about their route. What happened to Neal?"

"So, the facts are that he was involved in a scuffle on the

ship somewhere south of San Diego. An officer was killed. Neal and three other sailors are now AWOL, all suspects in the murder."

It took Mr. Maxwell a moment to process the information. "I don't believe it. I mean, I only met him briefly, but he doesn't seem like the kind of young man who would do something like that."

"Nobody around here believes it much, either. But one never knows what pressure a man is under. At sea, in the military, packed like sardines on a ship, officers bellowing orders? Stress is probably extremely high. Anyone could break under those conditions."

Mr. Maxwell responded with a blank stare, shaking his head. "That's just so hard to believe!"

"Yes, it is." Poland gave Mr. Maxwell his change, tipped his head, and said, "Have a blessed day!"

Have a blessed day. Somehow that didn't seem likely. The beautiful morning outside had lost its luster in the eyes of Veldon Maxwell. His plan had been to drive out to the Crowson home and visit with Neal's parents, letting them know that he still wanted Neal to play for the Pirates when his hitch in the Navy was over. Leaning against the corner post of the café porch, he gazed across the street, focused on nothing, wondering, *What now?*

Any loving parent with a child in such a position as Neal's would be overcome with worry. It seemed insensitive to visit them at a time when Neal's whereabouts were unknown and his safety in peril. Maybe, he thought, maybe he should just drive back to Shreveport and leave them be. Even to bring up his name might be too traumatic for them.

On the other hand, he thought, Neal loved baseball. Mr. Maxwell could sense it when they talked, see it when he was on the field. His talent was obvious, at least to anyone who was conscious. He was a true natural, gifted with the ability, born with the desire. A rare combination. "Mr. Baseball," he said under his breath. His parents were sure to know that better than anyone.

Maybe talking to someone who had a true admiration for Neal and his talent would be uplifting for them. It may be good, healing even, to redirect their attention to a time before the incident, to a time when he was at home, harassing his mom, doing chores with his dad, and playing baseball.

Let's do it! he told himself. With renewed energy, he was ready to go. Before stepping down off the porch, he checked the street for traffic. There were a few pedestrians and a couple of equestrians, but the only thing approaching was a mule-drawn wagon carrying a lone driver dressed in earth-stained cotton overalls and a thin, long-sleeved pullover shirt. *Farmer, I'll bet*, he thought. Striding to intercept the wagon, he hailed, "Excuse me, sir. Are you a resident here?"

"Fourteen years," bragged the man.

Offering a hand in greeting, he said, "Maxwell, Veldon Maxwell."

"Sam Boddie."

"Good to meet you, Mr. Boddie. I'm from out of town, and I was wondering if you might be able to give me directions to the Crowson home?"

"Which Crowson? There's several of 'em."

"Oh, goodness! That hadn't occurred to me." Mr. Maxwell

rubbed his forehead. He realized he didn't know the first name of either of Neal's parents. "Well, the parents of Neal Crowson."

Sam paused with a suspicious look, gazing down at Mr. Maxwell from his perch on the wagon bench. Who was this outsider, and why did he want to see Neal's parents? Not wanting to blatantly butt into Maxwell's business, he took a different approach. "You need some surveying done? Richard is the best surveyor in the South!"

"No, no. I represent the Shreveport Pirates baseball team, and we asked Neal to play for us before he went off and joined the Navy. I just want his parents to know we still want him to play for us when his hitch is over."

The explanation quelled Sam's suspicion. Relieved, he responded, "I see! Yeah, that boy is a natural athlete, for sure!"

"We think he is!" Maxwell continued, "I noticed the next stop south on the Louisiana & Northwest railroad is the community of Crowson. Is that where they live?"

"No," he responded. "There's a lot of Crowsons who live at Crowson. That's why they call it Crowson. Ha-har!" Sam was amused at his own wordplay. "But, ole Richard has to come to town a lot with his surveying stuff. He and Fannie live in a log house just south of Bienville, about two-and-a-half, three-mile. Nice place."

"Good! I look forward to seeing them."

"You come in on the train? Livery is right down the street if you need to rent a rig."

"Actually, I'm traveling in a motorcar and could be there in no time provided the road is in good shape. Would you know its condition?"

"Yes, it's good. Been too dry to have any mud, but it might be a bit rutted. Couple of low stretches that'll prob'ly be pretty rough, but I don't think you'll have any trouble getting through. Just follow the road south like I said, two-and-a-half to three miles."

"Thank you, sir!" Mr. Maxwell responded with a friendly salute.

Sam nodded, whipped the reins, and with a curt "Giddup!" urged the mule on again.

Mr. Maxwell plodded across the dusty road back to the alley where he had left his Pierce. The walk was short but still enough for a plump man to work up a sweat in the moist morning heat. He removed his Homburg and threw it in the back seat, followed soon thereafter by his sack coat. After a few turns on the crank handle, the engine jumped to life. He and the Pierce started south on the old dirt road.

Just out of town, the Louisiana and Northwest rail line curved west then south to run along the east side of the road. The rolling hills on either side were covered in farmland and pastures. Off in the distance were dense growths of shortleaf pines bordered with scattered cedar and sweetgums, while the bottomlands were lovely, open hardwood forests. It was a beautiful area of the state, and Mr. Maxwell enjoyed the ride.

It wasn't long before the pastures on the west side of the road gave way to pine savannahs. Soon, he got his first glimpse of the Crowson home, a large, log two-story with a well-manicured yard. To the south was the family garden; to the north, a barn, cow lot, and a small pasture, all wrapped by a pine thicket. Along the creek to the west were a sawmill and several outbuildings, no doubt sheltering tools, tack, and equipment needed around the homestead.

Mr. Maxwell thought it to be a pleasant and appealing setting, a fitting place for a young man such as Neal to have grown up learning the values of responsibility, duty, integrity, and the importance of a close-knit family. He turned the automobile off the road and drove right up to the front steps of the house.

Between Richard's business clients and his and Fannie's many grown children scattered around the parish, visitors were common at the Crowson home. But automobiles were still scarce. By the time Mr. Maxwell had closed the door of the Pierce, Richard had already stepped out onto the porch; Fannie was peeking through the screen door.

"Nice automobile," Richard said. "Don't get many visitors in automobiles."

"Thank you, sir. It's what I use for business when I have to travel some distance."

"Makes it nice, I guess."

"Yes, sir, it does. Would you be Mr. Richard Crowson?"

"That I would. Who might you be?"

"The name is Maxwell, Veldon Maxwell. I'm a scout for the Shreveport Pirates baseball team."

"Ah, yes, Mr. Maxwell." Richard's demeanor chilled, fearing another unwelcomed inquiry about Neal. "I think Neal mentioned you, but he's not here."

"Yes, I assumed. He told me he was going to join the Navy," he said to ease Richard's apprehension. "But I'm not here to see Neal. I'm actually here to talk to you. Not long, I'll only take a moment of your time."

Richard hesitated for a moment. "Okay. Come on up and join me on the porch."

Mr. Maxwell plodded up the steps to the porch, then followed Richard to a couple of chairs leaning against the wall between the front door and the porch swing. Flipping the chairs around, they sat half angled toward each other, half facing the road and across the fields beyond.

Richard wasted no time. "So, Mr. Maxwell, what can I do for you?"

With a serious look at Richard, he replied, "Well, as apparently you know, I talked with Neal last summer about coming to Shreveport to play for us." Richard, looking across the fields, nodded his head. "I saw him play several games and, I must say, I was very impressed with him. However, I was more impressed with his personality; humility, if you will."

Richard glanced up and said, "Thank you. He's a good young man."

"My opinion exactly. And it appears to be the opinion of the good citizens of Bienville as well, at least the ones that I spoke to."

Richard looked over at him, pausing only a moment before asking, "You talked to people in town?"

"Yes. Stayed the night there last night." Mr. Maxwell sat on the edge of the chair and turned toward Richard. In a lowered tone, he continued. "Look. I know Neal is in a bit of trouble. But the townsfolk don't believe the accusations. They believe in Neal, as do I."

Richard said nothing. He turned away and again stared across the fields. He had wondered what the local people truthfully thought. His friends had encouraged him, but that was to be expected. But if they defended Neal to a complete stranger, that has to be a genuine affirmation that they believed in him. The knowledge was comforting. He was touched.

Mr. Maxwell continued, "That is why I'm here to talk with you. I believe in Neal, and the Pirates believe in Neal. We would be honored to have him representing our team when he comes home from the Navy."

Richard nodded. "I thank you, sir. And I know you understand, of course, that I have no clue when he'll be back."

"Of course. But when he gets home, please tell him to get in touch with me."

"I certainly will. And thank you."

"Thank you!" Maxwell said. He stood and extended his hand to Richard. "I have faith that Neal's situation is going to turn out just fine."

Richard shook his hand and nodded but said nothing. He stood with his hands in his pockets and watched until Mr. Maxwell turned the Pierce onto the road and had driven out of sight.

Chapter 15: Escape Plan

The first rays of the sun peeked over the horizon. One found Neal's face and woke him from a restless sleep. He was anxious to get to the field so he could explore the stadium before any of the other players arrived. Neal turned to the business at hand. He put away the mattress and any other evidence of his presence.

After Benjamin delivered Katherine's message the previous night, he later returned with a bit of food for Neal's breakfast. The main kitchen was closed for the night, but he brought an apple, two biscuits, and a pint jar of sweet tea from his own stash. "Good job, Benjamin. Thank you," Neal whispered as he placed the food on the desk. Benjamin just nodded in return, then slipped out the door and pulled it shut as he left.

Neal stuffed the food into his pockets, picked up the tea jar, then exited through the window and slipped into the woods.

The main gate of the stadium was open. The groundsmen had gotten an early start and were pulling weeds along the fence lines. Neal explored the grandstands, careful to search every area for any gates, doors, or gaps that he could squeeze through. With each exit he found, he surveyed the adjacent areas and plotted the best escape routes into the surrounding neighborhoods. Each route must provide quick cover and no suspicious eyes or noisy dogs to give his location away. He'd have to check for those later.

The fence around the field was simple; a gate at first and third and another in deep center field. Center field was an easy exit with quick cover, but it was in view of every seat in the stadium. The first and third base gates were too close to the stands, and there would be a lot of pedestrians in those areas. The dugout doors led to exits under the bleachers; maybe that would work out somehow.

"James!" Coach Hill had arrived. "You're early today."

"Eager to work out the kinks, coach!" Neal smiled and exchanged pleasantries, delaying his search for a plan of escape until a more opportune time.

The other players filtered in over the next thirty minutes. Everyone knew the routine, so practice was practice, nothing out of the ordinary. Neal cooled off in the shade of the bleachers. Within a few minutes, most of the other guys had left the field.

"James!" Neal sat up and saw Coach Hill approaching. "I have a surprise for you!"

"A surprise?"

"Yes. Actually two."

"The more, the better!"

"Well, two is all you're gettin'."

"I feel blessed!"

Coach Hill laughed. "Okay, first is this glove. I figure you'd like to have one of your own, and this one is top quality and already broken in."

"Wow!" Neal examined the glove. "Thanks, coach! I've never had one this nice."

"Well, it's yours. And as I promised, here's a little advance for you; a hundred dollars. You'll still draw your pay next week with the rest of the team."

Neal took the five twenties from the coach's hand and stared at them. He was speechless for a moment, then looked up at the coach. "Thanks, coach. I—I wasn't expecting this."

"Ha! Don't worry; you'll earn it over the next few weeks!" Coach Hill grinned, then turned and walked away.

"Coach." Hill stopped and looked back at Neal. "I plan on staying here tonight. Is that okay?"

Coach smiled. "You can stay here for the rest of the season if you like. Unless we're on the road, or your performance goes to squat!"

Neal laughed, then responded, "Thank you, coach." With a smile, Coach Hill nodded, then turned and walked through the exit gate and out of sight.

"One hundred dollars! Whew!" Neal said to himself. It wasn't all that much, but it was more than he'd had in a while. And enough to keep him fed for a month if food was all he spent it on. For the most part, it just relieved the pressure of temporary privation; he now had a roof over his head and money for food and incidentals. He breathed a deep sigh of relief.

His new condition gave him peace of mind and a surge of energy. He got up and walked out of the stadium and began scoping out the surrounding blocks, looking for any available quick cover with suitable seclusion. After about an hour, he was back at the ballpark, where he plopped down on a bench in the shade, discouraged. West End Park was surrounded by houses and neighborhoods, except one small park that was well populated by children and their moms. Trying to escape through there would throw the patrons into a panic. There had to be another way, but it didn't look promising. Whenever the time comes, he resolved; he and Katherine would just have to make a decision and deal with the consequences.

Chapter 16: The Secret Service

"Senator, thank you for agreeing to visit with me on such short notice. I know this is an inconvenience, as your time is valuable."

"Not an inconvenience at all, Agent Clay. I welcome the opportunity to assist the Secret Service in any way possible."

"Thank you, sir. I trust the family is doing well?"

"Yes, no complaints presently. But that's nothing a bit of bad press can't change in a blink."

"No doubt!" Agent Clay agreed. "Some journalists just aren't worthy of the First Amendment."

The senator smiled and nodded his head, "True, and they prove that *so* often." They both chuckled.

"Senator," Agent Clay began, "Chief Wilkie and the entire agency appreciate your leadership here in Houston and in Washington as well. You seem to be an avid student of democracy and an enthusiastic advocate for your constituents."

"Thank you, sir."

"Oh, we thank you! Very much." Agent Clay began to pace the floor. "Your voting records, and might I add personal integrity, prove you to be very supportive of the law and law enforcement agencies both locally and nationally. And that includes agencies such as ours, the Secret Service. Your history proves you to be a person we can trust, which is one of the reasons I am here today."

"I appreciate that. How may I help you?"

"There is an issue of national concern that I wish to talk to you about. We highly suspect that a counterfeiting operation is centered here in your district."

"Counterfeiting?" Senator Bailey was surprised. "I had assumed you wished to question me about an AWOL sailor who's been seen in the area."

"AWOL sailor? Heavens, no, that's the Navy's business, not ours. I understand they use the help of independent agents and local law enforcement from time to time, but not our agency. I suppose if you have information pertinent to a case of theirs, we can easily relay the message to the Department of the Navy."

"I may have just that. There's more to the story than just a runaway sailor. My understanding is that an officer was murdered during the incident."

"That certainly changes the situation a bit, and I'll be glad to relay the information. However, my priority is my current assignment from the agency."

"Yes, of course."

"One of our main purposes, and I'm sure you know the reason the agency was formed, is to focus on the counterfeiting industry in the States. Specifically, we are tasked to track down and prosecute printers and distributors of counterfeit U.

S. currency of any kind."

"And you believe there is counterfeiting taking place in my district?"

"Yes. In fact, we think the counterfeiter is an acquaintance of yours."

Senator Bailey was shocked! He wasn't sure if Agent Clay was here to question him or to accuse him of being a co-conspirator. "I can assure you, Agent Clay, I know nothing of counterfeiting in my district. Or anywhere else, for that matter!"

"And I can assure *you*, Senator Bailey, we understand that. We've been on this case for quite some time. If I thought you were involved, I wouldn't be here without a warrant."

"I apologize. I'm—I'm just totally surprised by this news."

"I can see that, so let me reassure you; you are not a suspect. As I said, I am here because you've earned the trust of the agency."

"Thank you."

"Now, before I ask you any questions, let me tell you what we know. We know that you have somewhat of a political relationship with a certain Dr. George Akers."

"Dr. George?"

"Yes. He supported your run for senator in the past two elections."

"Yes, but he's not asked me for any favors or—"

"Not yet, senator. But please, let me continue." Agent

Clay wasted no time. "He has a medical office not too distant from the red-light district; an office where he treats brothel personnel and their patrons in a rather discreet manner, which I'm sure they appreciate. None of that is against the law—yet. It is understood that he owns a couple of these establishments and that he sees to it that none of his employees gives birth. I'm sure you understand what I mean. Again, that's not currently against the law, but it's definitely frowned upon as well as dangerous, unethical, and immoral. He's known to prescribe massive amounts of opiates for anything from a headache to a broken fingernail. That's not against the law.

"As you know, senator, there is strong national sentiment opposing these procedures and extreme pressure to outlaw all of them."

"Yes, that's correct."

"In addition, he's known for associating with scoundrels and rogues who live on the very rim of privilege and debauchery, a parasitic group, leaning one way or the other just enough to satisfy their needs. Some even have quite extensive criminal records. His actions and social relationships demonstrate the type of leech he is, except for his relationship with you."

Senator Bailey just nodded his head.

"Many in this crowd supported your senatorial campaigns, am I not correct?"

"Yes, but that is what Dr. George does for me," Senator Bailey replied. "On my own, I have no association with that crowd, none at all! But Dr. George, being somewhat a part of that group, can bring those votes to me. I do nothing, nor promise anything, that I don't commit to for all my constituents. He is a cad, and my daughter is quick to remind me of that. But despite his shady side, Dr. George has some redeeming qualities. He is quick to lend any help I might need, whether it be in a campaign, organizing a rally, or providing funds to a charitable cause anywhere in the Houston area. He's an excellent raconteur and has a wonderful sense of humor, which are minor things, I know. But he's always been attentive and respectful to my family and me. I have always questioned his motives and suspected that his conduct has been for his own personal benefit. Regardless, my experience with him has been honorable, albeit utilitarian."

"Our investigation has proved all of this to be true, senator."

"Your investigation? Of me?"

"Certainly, senator. I told you that the agency had done its research. You don't think I would discuss any information with you without verifying your character?"

"Of course, Agent Clay. I guess the word 'investigation' just caught me off guard."

"Ah, yes. It's a very common word in our business. In fact, the success of the Secret Service—"

"Father," Katherine blurted out as she stepped into the library. She stopped in her tracks when she saw the stranger talking with her father. "Oh! Please excuse me. I didn't realize you had a visitor."

"Katherine, this is Mr. Clay, an associate visiting from Washington. Mr. Clay, my daughter Katherine."

Agent Clay nodded, "Pleasure to meet you, Katherine."

"My pleasure, Mr. Clay. Sorry to burst in on you." Turning her attention to the senator, "It appears you two are in deep conversation, so I'll just see you when you're free."

"Yes, ma'am," the senator agreed.

"Nice to meet you, Mr. Clay."

"And you as well, Miss Katherine."

Katherine stepped through the doorway and closed the door fast behind her. Suddenly she froze in alarm. *'The success of the Secret Service'? Did he say Secret Service?* She had to know what was going on. Placing her ear close to the door, she strained to hear every word.

"You were saying, Agent Clay?"

"Yes. We had to verify your character before discussing any information with you. The success of the Secret Service, not to mention the survival of the nation's economy, demands stealth and confidentiality. I follow the measures established by the agency, whether I'm investigating you, Dr. Akers, or President Roosevelt himself."

"I understand, Agent Clay."

Agent Clay? Secret Service? Katherine tensed with fear. She couldn't believe Father would betray her. He was surrendering Neal to the authorities! It was unforgivable! She was tempted to storm into the room and give them both the fury of her anger but stopped short as Agent Clay began to speak again.

"As for your relationship with Dr. Akers, it was imperative that I hear your characterization of the relationship, and I am satisfied with it. Which brings me to the reason for my visit."

Katherine leaned in closer, intent to understand every word spoken by the soft voices beyond the thick oak door.

All at once, her focus was shattered by the sound of footsteps coming from the kitchen. She escaped up the stairs, hoping she hadn't been observed eavesdropping. *Surely it was just the housekeeper*, she rationalized. But Katherine couldn't risk being caught listening in on Father's conversation, regardless of who it may have been. She entered her bedroom, closed the door behind her, and lay across her bed.

Her fears ran rampant. The timing couldn't have been worse! What was the reason for Agent Clay's visit? Was it Neal? Was it Dr. Akers? Was it something else entirely? Katherine was frantic with the fear that her father could be revealing Neal's whereabouts. How could he? Or was he? Her mind was reeling. One thing was certain; her opportunity to hear Agent Clay's reason was gone. She had no choice but to trust her father's judgment.

In the library, Agent Clay continues. "There seems to be a spate of counterfeit bills surfacing around the country, and most notably here in the Houston area. We've questioned many citizens locally who have been caught passing the bills, and the trail of information seems to lead us to your acquaintance, Dr. Akers."

"I would believe minor discretions, but counterfeiting? That's a federal crime!"

"That is correct. I must confess; we have yet to catch him actually printing or distributing the bills. But, with the resources we have in the area, it's only a matter of time." Agent Clay took a deep breath. "As a matter of formality, senator, I need you to tell me if you know, or have ever suspected, that Dr. Akers is involved in any aspect of the counterfeiting business."

"Of course not, never! I am totally aghast!"

"As I suspected, thank you." Agent Clay continued, "Since we have no concrete evidence, I can't have a warrant issued, arrest him, or search his business or private premises. I need a warrant to look for evidence of printing, distributing, or both. And this is what brings me to you."

"Okay. What do you need from me?"

"Anything that can justify a warrant. Anarchy, inciting a riot, theft, illegal sale of intoxicating liquors, public drunkenness, disturbing the peace, swindling, falsifying legal documents. I'm not particular, senator. Do you know of any such thing that we can pin on him?"

"I'm sorry, but I don't. I've heard things, of course, but discounted them. As you know, those of us in positions of prominence or power are invariably the objects of jealousy or anger."

Agent Clay was resolute. "What kind of things have you heard? From whom?"

"Mostly, just things said in random conversations."

"Such as?"

"Well, such as," Senator Bailey pauses to think, "such as providing opium to the ladies in Happy Hollow...a local red-light district. I've heard about the abortions you referenced earlier. And even, horridly enough, ending the life of a baby or two at full-term birth. I can't fathom that, though. I can't see Dr. Akers doing anything like that."

"Who did you hear that from?"

"Katherine. A friend of hers who worked for him told her that. It's also common knowledge that he makes advances to the ladies, and the word is that this friend quit just to avoid his advances. That's why I discarded the information as just some drivel from a sour employee."

"Full-term birth? If he did that, it would constitute murder. Did she say anything else?"

"Uhm," he paused for an instant, "yes, yes she did. Earlier, you mentioned falsifying documents. This young lady said she found a few files in his records office containing personal identification records. She said she browsed through them, and it appeared that some were records of showing that he had changed people's names and identities."

"Could be legal. Could be illegal."

"True. I'm sorry, Agent Clay, but that's about all I can remember."

Clay paced the floor. "Alright, we have a few items I can investigate. But in the meantime, I need you to watch your interactions with him, and let me know if you see or hear of anything, anything that I can use to obtain a warrant."

"I'll be glad to. I still can't believe he's involved with counterfeiting, or really, that I haven't had the vaguest clue. I feel like such a fool!"

"Men like Akers are good at what they do. That's why so many get away with it. They're smart. Dirty, but smart."

Agent Clay stepped toward the door of Bailey's office, then paused. "Oh. What was it you wanted to tell me—something about an AWOL sailor?"

"Oh, yes," Senator Bailey replied. "As I was saying, an officer of the Great White Fleet was killed when the seamen, supposedly four of them, abandoned ship along Baja California just south of San Diego. Jumped off the ship right into the ocean. One of the sailors drowned, the other three escaped. One of those who escaped was Petty Officer Neal Crowson. My daughter and I met him in Hampton Rhodes at the exposition ball before the Fleet departed. He was a fine young man, or so it seemed; well-educated and very respectful to both my daughter and me. I find it hard to believe that he would commit such an act. In fact, he claims he was knocked overboard when trying to stop the brawl between the officer and the seamen."

"So, you've talked to him?"

"No. But it seems my daughter has." Agent Clay stood still, waiting for further explanation. The senator continued, "Somehow he made his way from California to Houston. He told her the story. I suspect that he occasionally stays in one of our outbuildings," the senator confessed. "It's a storage building, and most of the items have been in there for years. I can't remember the last time we moved anything, either in or out. So, it's the perfect place for someone to hide out."

"Have you contacted the authorities?"

"As I said, I just recently suspected it. I'm not quite sure who to contact or the best way to go about it."

"Does he come in and out regularly, meaning with any noticeable pattern?"

"No. I'm not even sure how many times he's been here."

"How many times have you seen him?"

"Well, fact is, Agent Clay, I haven't seen him."

"You haven't?"

"No, but I know he's been here. I've picked up on the clues."

"What kind of clues?"

"Primarily, it's the fact that my daughter has been making much more frequent visits to the storage building of late. She claims she's looking for an old dress or some such nonsense. But when we met Petty Officer Crowson at the exposition ball, Katherine was quite taken by him. Actually, he physically defended her from an overzealous scoundrel and won her favor." Senator Bailey paused a moment. "I'm afraid she fell head-over-heals for him, and I'm concerned that she may be giving him aide."

"That could be a problem." Agent Clay paused. "Since the sailor was not the primary reason for my visit, I'll have to get the facts on his case and let the chief give me instruction."

"I'll be glad to give you any aid you need."

"I must admit, the most likely scenario is that Chief Wilkie will have me pass your information to the Department of the Navy and request that they handle the situation. However, you may get public credit for the sailor's capture."

"Agent Clay, considering his relationship with my daughter, it would be better if your source remained anonymous. I don't need public praise that causes domestic division."

"I understand completely, senator." Agent Clay walked toward the door. "For the time being, don't do anything. I'll get back to you."

"I'll be waiting."

"Thank you for your time, senator."

"Thank you, sir."

Katherine worried all evening about the information her father might be sharing with Agent Clay. If only she hadn't left the door in such a rush, maybe she could have heard more. But she knew she didn't have a choice. Father would be furious if he learned she had been eavesdropping on an important conversation. Especially one with law enforcement, with an agent of the Secret Service.

But wondering about the details of that conversation haunted her well into the night. Frustrated and exhausted, she finally told herself, "I have to warn Neal. Whether I trust Father or not, I must tell Neal. If we don't develop a plan, we're sunk." The Buffalos were playing out of town, so Neal wouldn't be back for a couple of days. There was nothing she could do but wait. And waiting was torture. Her last thoughts as she nodded off to sleep were, *I have to tell Neal. We have to make plans. If we don't, we're doomed. I must tell him. Then, whatever happens...happens.*

Chapter 17: Love Recognizes Love

The Buffalos played well in the next few games, and Neal was a standout in every game. He was pleased with his performance and would expect no less of himself. But the more attention he gained, the more concerned he became about being recognized. It was a long shot to cross paths with anyone he knew, especially since most of his travels were in baseball parks far from northwest Louisiana. But he knew it was possible. And as the playoffs narrowed down to the final teams, the crowds got bigger, and his chances of being recognized increased. It made him somewhat uneasy, but he still bet against the odds. *The feds have probably moved on to other things*, he told himself. *Probably not even searching for me anymore*. But down deep, he didn't believe it.

The Buffalos headed back to Houston for a five-day break before the championship game on Saturday. Neal was glad the game was to be played at home in West End Park, the newest and most modern park in the Texas League. They would be facing a tough opponent in the Oklahoma City Indians. The Indians were in their first year with the Texas League and one of only two teams in the league that was not located in Texas. It had been a long season for the Buffs; 152 games with a record of 105 wins, 47 losses. This final game would be the icing on the cake.

Upon arrival at West End Park, Coach Hill called everyone to attention. "Five-day break, boys, and you know what that means...sleep in tomorrow." Cheers went up from all the players, as they were tired from travel. Then, with a smile, he added, "Get rested, 'cause practice starts at 1 p.m. Don't be late!" The cheers soon changed to grumbles and moans. "And Tuesday through Thursday, we'll practice twice a day." More groans.

One of the players asked, "Coach, don't we even get one day off?"

Coach laughed. "Okay, listen. If practice each day goes well, you can have Friday off to rest." Cheers again. "And I mean rest! Nothing strenuous. Clear your minds and give your muscles time to recoup...unless some of you want a short batting practice. Just let me know."

One of the players joked, "Oh, yes! We'll definitely let you know, coach!" A few of the guys chuckled, including Coach Hill, but most just smiled, quiet with fatigue. Everyone gathered their own gear and stowed it away in the locker room.

Exhausted but in good spirits, they left the park looking forward to a night in their own bed, except for Neal. His bunk was in the locker room. He longed to see Katherine, to let her know he was back in town, and to make some plans for the coming week. But it had been a long day, and he needed rest. He convinced himself that the wisest option was to get a good night's sleep so he could survive practice tomorrow. He would have to see Katherine after practice.

Morning came earlier than he was prepared to meet it. Noises from outside woke him up just after 8 a.m. He stumbled over to the locker room door and cracked it open enough to catch the blinding light of the midmorning sun and the noisy banter of the field prep crew. After taking a few seconds to acclimate himself, he dressed and stepped out into a warm, humid morning.

"Thought you were going to sleep 'til supper!" teased one of the groundsmen.

"Wish I could. I think some guy named Hill is trying to kill me." They laughed.

"Speaking of Hill, he had some coffee and breakfast treats dropped off a little while ago." The groundsman nodded toward the food.

"Well, bless his heart!" Neal teased.

"Bless it!" the groundsman repeated. "I think it was all for you, but we had to sample it. Ha!"

"Well, I guess if you're not sick by now, it must be safe for me."

Neal poured some coffee, ate a couple of boiled eggs, and grazed on the fruit and muffins. He decided to make a loop around the ballpark to walk his food down. The mild breeze felt good, and the action and songs of the birds made the walk pleasant. It was already getting hot, and the cup or two of water at the end of his walk tasted divine. Practice would start in a couple of hours, so Neal decided to climb to the upper level of the grandstands to find a seat in the shade and enjoy the breeze. It would allow time to rest and would also serve as a great time for him to ponder his predicament.

He had yet to come up with an escape plan, and the window to freedom was getting closer. Or maybe it was closing. There may be no way to escape. Just maybe he would get caught. But there's always the chance that the feds had stopped looking for him, and if so, he could just walk away after the game Saturday. Or return to the team next year or go back home to resume his previous plans. It was possible he could even go back to the Navy, explain what happened, and go back to his position on the ship. Or go to jail.

Neal became frustrated at his lack of clarity on the options, and his thoughts drifted back to Katherine. Maybe she would have a plan, an idea, or a practical option. He leaned forward and rested his chin in his hands, trying to clear his mind. The only thing he knew for sure was that he had to see her.

A little after noon, Neal put on his practice uniform. He was lacing up his cleats when some of the other players started drifting in to dress out. He engaged them in a little small talk, then walked out of the locker room to get a drink of cool, clean water from the water tap. He was glad the city had recently transferred the water line from Buffalo Bayou to the city's new artesian system. It was much better than the water supply in other parts of Houston, but the city was hard at work trying to get clean water to all areas of town.

As he turned from the water tap, he saw a gentleman approaching. He looked to be around forty years in age, was carrying a notepad, and was well dressed except for the large, wide-brimmed hat on his head. "Good afternoon!" the man said as he stretched out his hand.

"Yes, it is," Neal responded as he gripped and shook the man's hand.

"I'm Ben Tidwell, reporter for the Beaumont Enterprise. You must be the new guy, Landis. James Landis. I know most of the other players on the team."

"Yes, sir, nice to meet you." Neal became nauseous. He

knew there would be a lot of press at the game, but it had never occurred to him that reporters would attend the practices.

"I've heard a lot about you. You have a very intriguing story, showing up at just the right time as you did. I'd like to do a feature on you, tell your story, if you don't mind."

"Uh, maybe after the championship. I'd like the focus to remain on the team right now."

"Okay, I understand. Later then," Tidwell replied. "Looking forward to seeing you on the field."

"I hope I don't disappoint," Neal quipped. He tipped his cap and walked toward the field, stopping at the edge of the shadows under the grandstands. It was still early, but there appeared to be more than a hundred people in the stands. He searched the faces to see if he recognized anyone, and to his relief, he didn't.

Pat walked up beside Neal. "It's going to be a zoo out here."

"I didn't realize…."

"Don't worry about it. Mostly just local fans here to watch; a few reporters and maybe a couple of scouts."

"Are they always here?"

"They are for the championship games. It's their business, you know, building the excitement. Some are also watching the Indians practice over at Westmoreland Park."

Neal nodded, trying to wrap his head around the implications.

"Ah, don't sweat it," Pat said. "The way I look at it,

reporters and scouts are just fans with more interesting jobs." They stood silent for a moment, then Pat added, "Let's go warm up!"

Practice lasted about two hours. Coach Hill wanted the players to get a workout, but not worn out. Reporters approached several of the players, but Neal took a discreet path to the locker room to clean up and change clothes. He walked out of the stadium and slipped through a small group of fans lingering outside the stadium entrance on Andrews Street.

"Excuse me, suh." Neal heard the call, but he kept walking. "Excuse me, suh!" He realized the call was meant for him. "Suh, I used t' play ball, and I'd like to ax you a queshion." He risked a quick glance. It was Benjamin!

At once, he composed himself. "Yes? How can I help you?"

Benjamin extended his hand down the street. "Don't mean'a slow you, sir. We can walk." They resumed walking down the street until they were well away from the fans. In a low voice, Benjamin said, "Miss Katherine sent me for you."

Neal smiled. "She knows I'm in town, then?"

"Yessuh," Benjamin said with a nod. "D'ese days she keeps tabs on d'em Buffs," he said smiling, "on you, I'd say." Then he added, "Da Model K is down da street a bit so's not to be noticed."

"Lead on."

He was very anxious to see Katherine, so the moderate drive from the stadium to the senator's house seemed to take forever. A couple of blocks before they reached their destination, Benjamin pulled over to the curb. "You best stay under da woods from here," he instructed.

"Good idea." Neal stepped out of the car.

"I'll let Miss Katherine know you's here right after I put away da Model K."

"You're the best!" Neal replied. Benjamin smiled and nodded, then eased the car into motion and headed toward home. Neal stood at the edge of the road for a moment and watched him drive away. He strolled down the street, scanning the area to make sure there were no spectators. When comfortable that he hadn't been noticed, he slipped out of sight and made his way to his hideout in the woods beside the house.

He found a comfortable spot in the storeroom to sit and wait for Katherine. It was a good spot, not too close to the window, but with a clear view of the house. About a half-hour passed before he saw Katherine crossing the yard. As always, he smiled at the sight of her. But something was different. By the pace of her walk and the look on her face, he knew something was wrong. He met her as she entered the door.

She threw her arms around him and whispered, "Neal!" She held him tight, so tight that it was difficult for him to close the door.

"Katherine, is everything alright? You seem worried."

She looked into his eyes, doubting her decision, but soon yielded. "I was reluctant to tell you, but after much deliberation, I feel I must."

"What on earth?"

"There was a Secret Service agent here a couple of days

181

ago, asking Father all kinds of questions."

"About me?"

"I don't know. I was looking for Father, and when I walked into the library, they were engaged in a serious conversation. They stopped talking immediately when I barged in."

He stepped back and held her by the shoulders. "What did they say?"

"Well," her gaze wandered as she tried to recall the events, "as I entered, I heard the agent say, 'Secret Service,' but then they stopped talking. Then Father introduced him as Mr. Clay. I excused myself from the room, but when I closed the door, I tried to listen to their conversation." She turned her gaze back to his. "All I heard clearly was Father call him 'Agent Clay,' the name 'Dr. Akers,' and some mention of verifying Father's character before sharing information."

"Sharing information? What information? What did you hear?"

"Not much, really. I heard footsteps in the kitchen and had to flee to my bedroom."

"But what, exactly, *did* you hear?"

"Well, Agent Clay told Father that he was satisfied with Father's relationship with Dr. Akers. Then he said, 'Which brings me to the reason for my visit.' And that's when I heard the footsteps. I had to run upstairs to keep from being discovered!"

"So, you never heard the real reason for his visit?"

"No. I'm so worried, Neal!

Neal held her close, consoling her as best he could while pondering the situation. He remained composed, calm, cognizant of the implications but not assuming the worst. Optimism was a trait inherited from his mother, who never seemed to fear any tribulation. He'd often heard her say, "Ninety percent of the things people worry about never happen." And she was right.

Neal led Katherine to the old desk in the storeroom office where they both sat, side by side. Holding her hands, he summarized the facts. "Okay, here is what we know. Agent Clay met with your father and discussed his relationship with Dr. Akers. He investigated your father and said he was satisfied with his relationship with Dr. Akers. He was satisfied enough that he would disclose information to your father. Then he was about to get to the point. Right?"

"Yes."

In a matter of fact, encouraging manner, Neal postulated, "Then it sounds to me like Agent Clay has some dirt on Dr. Akers."

Katherine turned to Neal, "Oh, Neal! Do you really think so?"

"I don't know, but that's what it sounds like. If not, why would he investigate your father and their relationship?"

Katherine's eyes grew wide with the revelation. "That's true! Why would he, unless he thought maybe Father was involved in Dr. Akers' shenanigans?"

"That's my thought exactly," Neal replied. "Except, I wouldn't have used the word 'shenanigans.'"

"You're crazy!" Katherine laughed as she jumped to her

feet. "So, it's not about you!"

"Well, let's not go that far. We don't know that for certain."

"Okay, okay. That's true."

"But most likely, I believe, Dr. Akers is in some deep trouble. You said yourself that he's a cad and does horrible things."

"Yes, he does!" Katherine said vehemently.

"Okay, we're going to go with that. But let's not let our guard down; we still have to be very careful."

"Absolutely! But I feel so much better now like a load has been lifted off my chest."

"Yes. And considering all, I feel much better than I did a few minutes ago."

Katherine stepped in front of Neal as he sat on the desk. She leaned into him and put her arms around his shoulders, holding him close and tight. He returned her warm embrace, savoring the faint, sweet scent of the perfume he had dreamed of while away. Neither of them spoke. It was enough to be present in the moment, to experience the warmth of love, to feel the faint, soft beating of another heart.

A few moments passed. She straightened up, placed her hands on his cheeks, and gave him a soft kiss. "Are you hungry?"

"In many ways," he smiled wryly, "but food would be the safest to pursue."

She swatted his shoulder. "You're such a—a schoolboy!" she laughed.

"Who, me? I just said I was hungry, that's all. Famished, actually."

"Mm-hmm!" She placed her hands on his shoulders and gave him a quick kiss. "Well, hungry man, I can get you some food from the kitchen if you're so famished."

Neal pulled her close. "Thank you, but I can't stay, and you don't need to draw any attention."

"Can't stay? Why not?"

"I need to get back to the clubhouse; practice is early. I'll buy something on the way back."

She held him close and whispered, "I don't want you to leave."

"Believe me, I don't want to go," he replied. Again, they stood in silence, each savoring the closeness and warmth of the other. At last, Neal took a deep breath, then released it. "I have to go."

"No-o-o!" she protested and tightened her embrace.

"Look," Neal laughed. "Don't torture me! I have to go, although, I must say, I truly hate it!"

"Fine then," she pouted but continued to hold him.

He put his hands on her waist and stood to his feet. He stared into her eyes, deeply, as if to search the depths of her soul. "Have I told you that I love you?"

Katherine gazed back, a satisfied smile forming across her lips. "Not in so many words. I knew it, though."

"How did you know?"

"Grandmother used to say, 'Love recognizes love; it doesn't have to be spoken.' Personally, though, I think it's a wonderful thing to hear." She rose to her toes, held his cheeks in her hands, and pulled his lips to hers. Her soft, tender kiss captivated his soul. At that moment, his cares were forgotten; his predicament was nonexistent. She was his world, his life.

Soon, their lips parted. She peered deeply into his eyes and whispered, "That, sir, was my unspoken response." Smiling, she added, "But for your listening pleasure, I love you, too!"

...

Practice came early. Neal was up by 7 a.m., but to his surprise, there were already spectators scattered throughout the stands. *This is crazy*, he thought to himself. The Texas League was bigger than anything he had experienced before, and he found such interest in the playoffs to be unbelievable. The growing crowds at practices concerned him. He knew he would have to inspect the faces in the crowd every day, thoroughly but surreptitiously, of course.

Practices were held in a more relaxed atmosphere, and interaction between the fans and players happened more often than at an official game. Although, he thought he had heard somewhere that access to the players was limited to the press, scouts, and fans with connections. *That's not so bad*, he told himself. *I don't know any of those elites except Dr. George.*

He pondered about Dr. George for a while. Maybe Dr. George wouldn't be there. It was quite possible he could be arrested before the day of the game. If so, that would eliminate the only person he could think of that could identify him, even though he believed the chance of that happening was minute. They had met only once, half a year ago, in a very different venue. Neal was clean-shaven and in a military uniform at the ball. Now he had a short beard and would be wearing a baseball uniform. And would be under a different name. "Not a chance," Neal told himself.

Chapter 18: Katherine's Interrogation

"Whoa! Whoa, there," Benjamin instructed as the horse came to a stop at the front steps of the senator's house.

"Thank you, Benjamin," Katherine said. "That was a most pleasant ride." She grabbed her bags, exited the carriage, and hurried into the house.

"Kathrine?"

"Oh, Father! You must see the new hat I bought for the game. It's simply adorable!"

"Katherine, I need—"

"Look, Father," she said as she placed her new hat on her head. "Isn't it just divine?"

"Yes, certainly," he blurted. "Katherine, we must talk."

"Father, you haven't even looked at—"

"Katherine! Listen to me," the senator scolded. "Yes, the hat is lovely. But I need you to put it down and come into the library."

She placed her new hat on the table at the foot of the stairs. "Father, what on earth is the matter?"

The senator said nothing as he ushered Katherine into the library. He closed the door behind them, then turned and motioned to a parlor chair across the room. "Katherine, I believe you've met Agent Clay." Surprised, she glanced over and saw Agent Clay as he rose from his chair.

For a moment, she stood speechless, her mind racing. What had her father gotten her into? She collected her thoughts, "Yes, of course." She nodded a greeting in his direction, "Agent Clay."

"My pleasure, ma'am," he responded. Katherine felt that he was right; she certainly couldn't fathom how this was going to be any pleasure for her.

Turning her attention back to her father, she said, "What's this all about, Father?"

"Agent Clay has a few questions for you. He thinks, maybe, you may be able to provide some information on a case or two he's involved in."

A case or two? That doesn't sound promising. Katherine looked back to Agent Clay and tried to present an air of confidence and cooperation. "I'm not sure if I can be of assistance, but I'll do my best."

Agent Clay responded, "Thank you, Miss Katherine." He took a couple of steps in her direction. "Please, take a seat," he said as he motioned toward a chair. "I don't intend to keep you long, but whatever time I take, I'd like for you to be comfortable."

Katherine said nothing. She took a seat at the end of the nearby couch; her father sat on the other end. Agent Clay pulled his chair over and sat facing her.

"Katherine, I understand that you have, or have had, a friend or two who have worked for Dr. George Akers. Is that true?"

Katherine felt immediate relief. *It's about Dr. George*, she thought. Her distaste for Dr. George renewed her confidence; she'd be glad to see that old devil locked away. But she wondered if her father felt the same way. She chanced a look at him to read his demeanor.

"It's alright, Katherine. Tell him what you know."

She looked back at Agent Clay. "Yes, sir. Actually, three of my friends have worked for him."

"What information have they told you about Dr. Akers or the activities in his clinic? For example, the office atmosphere, medical procedures, clientele, other businesses operating from within the clinic—anything along those lines."

She paused a moment, forming her words with caution. It had never been her nature to gossip or to spread hearsay. And even though she had a disdain for Dr. George, she found it difficult to voice her friends' accusations. But she felt she had no choice. Tactfully, she began. "Well, all of them found it difficult to work there." She paused, not wanting to get into specifics.

Agent Clay pursued, "Okay. Why did they find it difficult?"

Katherine glanced at her father again. He nodded, reassuring her that it was okay to answer. "Honestly, sir, Dr. Akers is not a faithful husband. He's quite aggressive towards women, especially the young, lovelier ones. He can be very unpleasant. Even threatening."

"Is this something that your friends have told you directly, or is it your experience as well?"

She paused, shot a glance at her father, then confessed, "All of us, sir." Senator Bailey understood the implication; he said nothing but noticeably shifted in his seat.

"I'm sorry," sympathized Agent Clay. "How did your friends respond to him?"

"They all quit working for him. They told me, all three of them, that he would make crude remarks and attempt to—" Katherine flashed a quick glance at her father then back to Agent Clay, then to the floor, "attempt to touch them inappropriately. Sometimes succeeding before they could react. But eventually, they all resigned. Only one stayed more than just a few weeks."

Agent Clay scratched a few notes on his notepad. The sound of his scribbling seemed to echo off the walls. Katherine thought it was a ghastly sound. It was eerily reminiscent of women's college, of her only time in the principal's office for disciplinary action where she had a mere verbal disagreement with an instructor's opinion. She had feared she would be expelled and sent home an abject failure, ashamed to face her parents. Father was adamant that discipline and respect be practiced at all times.

Her reverie was interrupted by Agent Clay. "In what capacity were they employed?"

"Excuse me?"

"What jobs did your friends have at the clinic?"

"Oh." Her thoughts were whisked back to the present moment. "Two were receptionists, at different times, of course. The other managed the business affairs of the office.

She was the one who worked there the longest. But that was only about six months."

"Does his medical staff rotate in and out that quickly?"

"Oh, no," Katherine replied. "His relationship with his medical staff is strictly business. It's strange," she continued, "the medical staff has no interaction with the clerical staff, except one employee who brings paperwork to the office for billing. It's a rather intimidating atmosphere in the clinic. And the clerical staff is not allowed in the clinical area."

"Hmm. It could be to keep the area sterile, to keep infection at a minimum." He jotted down a few more notes. "If the conditions were so bad in the clerical office, why did your one friend stay so long, if you can classify six months as 'long'?"

"Her husband was in Cuba with the Army; she needed the job. But early on, she had set Dr. George strait. She let him know that his advances would stop, or her husband would pay him a visit when he returned to the States."

Looking at his notepad, Agent Clay commented, "Her husband must have returned, then, since she left the clinic."

"Oh, no. She left because of what she saw! She was frightened!"

Agent Clay and the senator both sat bolt upright, startled at her remark, "Frightened?" Clay asked. "What did she see?"

Katherine looked from Agent Clay to her father, then back to Agent Clay. "She—she had to use the lavatory, but somehow the door was locked from the inside. She knew the clinic was off-limits, but her," she continued delicately, "her situation was urgent, and the nursing staff had all gone. So, she decided to use the clinic lavatory." She paused.

"Get to the point, Katherine," the senator instructed flatly.

"She had to make her way past the exam rooms to get there. As she was tiptoeing down the hall, she heard some voices coming from the exam room just ahead of her. She slipped up to the door and peeked into the room just as Dr. George was placing stacks of money into a satchel."

Agent Clay and the senator exchanged glances. Katherine continued, "She said it was tons of money. Thousands, tens of thousands, possibly even a hundred thousand dollars."

Agent Clay thought for a moment, then asked, "Were the bills loose or bundled?"

"Bundled. Lots of bundles. And they were neat and flat like they were fresh from the bank."

"Katherine," the senator stated, "Dr. George is a wealthy man, you know."

"That's what I told her. But she was afraid because it was so much money, and she thought probably she had witnessed a dirty deal of some sort."

Agent Clay interjected, "Dirty deal? What made her think that? Was someone else in the room?"

"Yes, that's what scared her more than the hoard of money. There was a sleazy, unsavory fellow in a dingy black suit with his hair slicked back. She said he looked like a gangster, or an anarchist, or hoodlum. He frightened her. She said he gave her the chills."

"Did either of them see her?"

"She doesn't think so, but she said she wasn't going to stay and find out. She tiptoed out of the clinic and never went back."

"When was that?"

"About three or four months ago. April, maybe March."

"What is her name? I need to speak to her."

Kathrine panicked. "No, Agent Clay! I swore I would never tell!"

"I understand, Miss Bailey. But this could be bigger than you can even imagine, even a matter of life or death. For her safety, and possibly yours, I need to speak with her. It is of considerable national concern."

She looked over at her father, hoping he had an alternative plan. But he offered nothing. She turned back to Agent Clay. "Is there another option? I realize the gravity of the situation, but I *promised* her I wouldn't tell."

"If I had one, I would definitely offer it."

Katherine exhaled in exasperation as her gaze dropped to the floor. There was no open path to take, no hidden door to escape through. *Father wants me to tell*, she told herself, *and I know it's because he's concerned for my safety*. It took a few moments to convince herself, but in the end, she decided there was no better option.

"Her name is Beth McHue," she confessed. She felt defeated. "She'll hate me until the day she dies!"

"Maybe," replied Senator Bailey. "But without your help, that could happen prematurely." Katherine cast a tearful gaze at her father. His message was clear, and she knew he was right. But at the moment, it didn't help much.

Agent Clay broke the silence, "Beth McHue. Is Beth a nickname?"

"Elizabeth," Katherine responded.

"I know the family," the senator said. "I can give you the address and any other information you need."

"Thank you, senator." Turning his attention back to Katherine, Agent Clay began again, "Are you okay, Miss Bailey?" She just nodded her head. "I assure you your information is the very best option for the good of the case and for the safety of Mrs.—," he glanced down at the paper for a reminder, "Mrs. McHue."

Without feeling, she responded, "Thank you. May I go now?"

"Not just yet," he replied. "There's another matter we need to discuss, but I'll try not to keep you long." She stared at the floor, emotionally spent and mentally exhausted. She had no idea what more she could tell him. All she wanted was to hide in her room. Agent Clay continued, "Miss Bailey, I need to ask you about Petty Officer Neal Crowson."

Katherine stood up straight, rigid as a soldier at attention.

Both men rose. "I'm sorry if I startled you," Agent Clay apologized.

Her body tingled from her head to her toes. She stared at Agent Clay, eyes wide and mouth agape. She couldn't speak, but she could think, and the realization landed heavily on her emotions. Spinning around, she cried, "Father! How could you!"

"Now, Katherine, you know I just want to do what is best."

Her blood boiled with anger, a reaction completely out of character for her. "You betrayed me, Father! You lied!" She felt a pang of regret as soon as the words had been uttered.

"Katherine! Calm down! I did not lie, and I did not betray you! Agent Clay came here to ask questions, and I gave him some answers. He is here to straighten this all out if that's at all possible. Give him a chance to do it!"

Katherine spun around and stomped to the door. She grabbed the knob intending to sling the door open but stopped in place and stood there, silent. There was so much to think about, so much to process, and she wasn't one often given to emotion. Yes, she was mad and hurt, and almost anyone would understand that. But she knew her father was right. Neal wouldn't want to be a fugitive the rest of his life, nor would he want to endanger her by taking her with him. The only practical choice was to clear his name. But how? As ingenious, resourceful, and astute as she was, that answer had remained thus far beyond her grasp. Perhaps her emotional attachment to Neal had blocked her clarity of thought, and maybe, just maybe, that was to Neal's benefit.

Releasing her grip on the doorknob, she turned to face the men. With a deep sigh, she spoke stoically, "What is it you wish to know?"

Both men knew she wasn't happy, but they were glad she had decided to cooperate. "Please, Katherine, come sit," the senator said, motioning to her previous position on the couch. Surrendering to the inevitable, Katherine trudged over and sat on the couch.

Agent Clay began, "First, let me tell you that my priority is Dr. Akers, not Petty Officer Neal Crowson. He's the Navy's business. But as a federal agent, I'm obligated to provide any other federal agency with the information I discover pertinent to their operation. You can understand that, can't you?"

Katherine nodded her head.

"I have no qualm with Crowson. But I know he doesn't want to be a fugitive for the rest of his life, and I don't think you want that either. That's no future for either of you." He paused, allowing Katherine to ponder the gravity of his remarks. Then he continued in a more familiar, compassionate tone, "What I want is to give Neal the opportunity to clear himself with the Navy, and the way to do that is to let him tell his story. That's the only chance Neal has, don't you agree?"

Katherine's eyes welled with tears, but she knew Agent Clay was right. She lifted her gaze to his and softly replied, "Yes. I agree."

"Thank you, Katherine," Clay replied. "You'll not regret that decision." Katherine nodded, kneading her hands as if she doubted his words.

He continued, "Okay. The senator has briefed me on your history with Officer Crowson: where you met, the exposition ball, his defending you from an aggressor, your time together until he set sail with the Fleet." Choosing his words with discretion, he continued, "He also informed me of the incident on the ship involving the death of an officer and Crowson's subsequent...escape from the ship around San Diego." He paced, rubbing his chin with his fingers as if in deep thought. "The senator also tells me that, occasionally, Crowson has been visiting you here. Is that true?"

Katherine sent a disappointed glance at her father, then looked down at the ornate Bigelow rug. "Yes," she replied.

"Is he staying here now?"

"No."

"What is your recent interest in the storage building outside?"

Katherine's stare shot up to her father, her anger rising again. It was apparent that her father had revealed everything to Agent Clay, at least everything that he knew. *What's the use?* she thought. If Neal was to be exonerated, the truth had to be told. She capitulated, "Neal has spent the night there a few times."

"I thought you said he wasn't staying here?"

"He's not! At least, not since…."

Agent Clay prodded, "Since?"

After a short pause, Katherine answered, "Since he's been playing for the Buffalos."

Senator Bailey looked shocked. He glanced at Agent Clay then back to Katherine.

Agent Clay asked, "The who?"

"The Buffalos, Houston's professional baseball team. He happened to be watching a practice of theirs when one of the players got hurt. He offered to fill in for the duration of the practice session and apparently made an impression. He's now a starting outfielder for them." The men stared at her, dumbfounded. She continued, "He's staying in the locker room under the stadium, at least until the championship game is over."

Agent Clay jotted his notes again. He paused for a moment,

tapping his pencil on the notepad. Then he asked, "Isn't he afraid he'll be recognized?"

"No, but I am." She sighed. "He says no one will be there that he knows. And the whole team thinks his name is James, James Landis. They don't know that he is," she sat up straight and proud, "that his real name is Petty Officer Neal Crowson!"

Clay jotted the alias in his notes. He turned his attention back to Katherine. "And you don't agree that he won't be recognized? Why?"

"Well, because Dr. George will be there. I suppose Father told you that Dr. George was seated at the table with us at the exposition ball. He and Neal spoke that night, albeit briefly. But Dr. George is good with names and faces, and that concerns me."

"And it doesn't concern Neal?"

"Neal says the ball was half a year ago, and they only spoke briefly that one night." She added, "He also says Dr. George will only see him from a distance and that his new beard will make recognition even more difficult."

"So, Neal has a beard now?"

"Yes. It's not long, but it is quite dark and thick. And his hair is longer too."

Agent Clay stood and began pacing the floor again. Katherine was quite surprised that her father had remained so quiet during the questioning. Usually, he was the man in charge at inquisitions and meetings. She was impressed at his resolve to allow Agent Clay to lead as he saw fit and for allowing her to answer without interruption, correction, or additional information.

Just a few steps in front of Katherine, Clay's pacing stopped. "When is this championship game?"

"Saturday."

"Hmm, three days." He stood still, rubbing his chin again, processing the thoughts that were racing through his mind. Neal, Dr. Akers, murder, counterfeiting, only three days to plan…. Changing directions abruptly, he asked, "How do you know Dr. Akers will be there?"

"He never misses the home games, and certainly not the playoffs," Katherine replied. "I've heard he has some level of financial investment in the club. Probably gambling on the games as well if I had to guess."

Clay nodded, then sat down facing her, placed his elbows on his knees, and clasped his hands, fingers threaded together. He looked up at her and, in a very serious tone, said, "Miss Katherine, it is of *utmost* importance that you tell no one of this meeting, especially Neal. Doing so would only make conditions and consequences worse for him. Neither of us wants that, do we?" She glanced back down to the rug and shook her head 'no.'

He continued, "He needs to stay the course, play the game. Change nothing unless he hears from me. That's the only way we can take any steps to help him. Can you see that?" Once again, she just nodded. "Thank you, Miss Katherine. I think that will be all for now." He stood and, in the fashion of a gentleman, extended a hand to help her up from the couch.

Senator Bailey stood at the same time and said, "Thank you, Katherine. We'll talk later." Katherine didn't look at him. She responded with pursed lips and a slight dip of her chin, then exited the library and fastened the door behind her.

"Fine young lady!" Clay observed.

"Yes, she is. But at this particular moment, she's not a happy young lady."

Clay chuckled. "No, but she handled it all quite well. You wouldn't believe how horridly some people conduct themselves."

The senator quipped, "Apparently, you've forgotten where I work!" The humor was a refreshing break, and they shared a jovial laugh.

Agent Clay stood silent for a moment. "Senator, it occurs to me that if Dr. Akers never misses a game and Crowson plays for the team, then Saturday, we'll have both rabbits in the same cage."

"Yes w—*you* will," he said and smiled.

Clay had a faraway look in his eyes as if contemplating an intriguing thought. "That just may work to our advantage." He looked up at the senator, "I could focus on Akers and alert the Navy officials so they can handle the situation with Crowson. I need to brief Chief Wilkie. If he concurs, we could conceivably address both cases at the same time."

"That would be great, Agent Clay. Just tell me if I need to help or stay out of your way."

"Right now, I just need the information for Mrs. McHue. I'll send someone by to get her statement. My priority is to consult with the chief."

Chapter 19: A Plan

Benjamin waited at the rear door of the house, rotating his cap clockwise in his hands like a rolling tire. It was late in the afternoon on the Thursday before the big game. He had asked Subie to tell Katherine that he wanted to see her.

Soon the door opened wide. "Hello, Benjamin," Katherine said in a gay tone. "What can I do for you?"

In a hushed tone, not much more than a whisper, he replied, "Yes'm, I just had t' run an errand or two for da senator, and I happened t' end up over at West End Park. I know how coaches coach, you know, and dey don' like no players 'xpendin' too much energy on a day affore a big game." A big grin crossed his face, "So, I thought it'd be okay to bring you a souvenir from the park."

Katherine cocked her head in confusion and stared at him for a moment. Then her eyes grew wide, as did the smile on her face. "Thank you, Benjamin! I just love souvenirs!"

"Yes'm. Jus' ring me later, you know, so's I can make the return."

"Yes, I will. Thank you!" Katherine closed the door and went to her room to touch up her face and hair. Moments later, she crossed the yard and entered the storage building.

Neal met her as she shut the door. He embraced her and gave her a long, hungry kiss. Katherine offered no resistance. Their lips parted, and still holding her in his arms, he placed his cheek against hers. "I'm so glad to see you," he whispered.

She replied, "I didn't think I would get to see you before the game."

"Me neither." He leaned back and looked into her eyes. "We've been terribly busy, and the coach has put restrictions on our off time. He finally gave us free time this afternoon until curfew at 8 p.m. I didn't think I was gonna have time to get here and back until Benjamin showed up."

Smiling, Katherine held him close again and rested her head on his chest. "That Benjamin! He's looked after me since I was in primary school."

"And I'm sure you've kept him *extremely* busy, the poor soul!"

"You hush," she said as she reared back and smacked him on the shoulder, "or I'll have him cart you back to your—your cell under the bleachers!"

Laughing, Neal pulled her back into his embrace. He leaned back against the door, shifted his hands to her waist, and gazed deep down into her eyes. Her inhibitions escaped her, evaporating like a warm breath on a cold morning. She pressed against him boldly, without shame, wanting nothing but to savor every intimate moment. "Let me tell you something, young lady. I can guarantee you this," he said, "neither Benjamin nor wild horses or a chain hooked to your father's Ford Model K could pull me away from you right now."

Katherine began to sense a shift in her vision. For the first time in her life, she was able to look deep into the eyes of another human being, to focus beyond the lashes, the lenses, and the color. The sparkle in his eyes seemed to change from a reflection on the surface to a flickering fire that radiated from somewhere deep within his soul. And as the flames passed from his heart to hers, she began to get a warm feeling all over, a sense of security, peace, and hope.

She said nothing but stretched up to press her lips to his, her heart to his, and her soul to his.

They spent a while in silence, contented, like the silence between those who are at peace with each other, fully familiar, totally trusting.

Katherine broke the silence, "I need to tell you something."

Neal leaned back to look at her. "This doesn't sound good."

"I'm not supposed to tell you, but I need to tell you."

"Not supposed to?"

"They know about you."

"Who knows about me?"

"The Secret Service. They know you're in Houston, and they know you come here, to this house." Neal stepped back from her, staring at her in disbelief. Katherine clutched his hands. "They know you play for the Buffs."

Neal spun around and began pacing the floor, rubbing his forehead as if it would help him clear his mind. He turned back to Katherine. "How? How did they find out?"

"Father said—"

"Your father called them?"

"No! No, it's not like that! Agent Clay met with Father about Dr. George. They suspect him of some sort of crime against the government. But Father thought he came to ask questions about you, and it kind of slipped out."

"Slipped out? It kind of slipped out?"

"I don't know exactly how it happened, but it did. The main thing is, Agent Clay said you're not the one he's after. He's after Dr. George for *his* crime if he can prove it. Not you."

"And you believe that?"

"Yes! He said the Secret Service doesn't concern itself in the affairs of the Navy. They focus on crimes against the country and the personal safety of the president." She rushed over to Neal and wrapped her arms around his waist. "When Father mentioned you, Agent Clay had no clue what he was talking about."

Neal put his arms around her shoulders and held her close. Resting his chin on the top of her head, he considered the options, which were few, and none seemed good. Soon, he muttered, "I could leave now, not even show up for the game."

Alarmed, Katherine countered, "No, Neal! Agent Clay said the best thing for you to do is to not change anything, to go on as if nothing has changed. Play the game, he said."

"The best thing? That's the best thing? I'll be a sitting duck!"

"He said there will be severe consequences if you run again. Neal, we can't run forever."

The word jarred him. He leaned back and stared at her. "We?"

"You don't think I'm going to give you up, do you? If you run, I run."

"I can't let you do that!"

"You have no choice," she said. "Either we leave here together, or we stay here together. And whatever happens, happens!"

"No!" He spun away from her and began to pace, his mind reeling in dread. "No! It's no good! I can't get you mixed up in this!"

She clutched his arm to stop his pacing. "I'm *already* mixed up in this. Don't you realize—"

Pulling away from her, he stormed toward the door. "I can't listen to this! You can't come with me, and that's final!"

Trailing behind him, she shouted, "Neal! Wait! It's the only way! Don't you walk out on me!" The words bounced off the back of the slammed door, echoing in the hollow surrounds of the suddenly quiet storage room.

Her vision blurred with tears. *How could he just walk out?* she asked herself. *Do I mean nothing to him? Was all this time together just a lie?* She stumbled into the inner room and plopped down on the desk, immersing herself in a dark replay of the preceding minutes. *Did I say something wrong or put too much pressure on him? Maybe I was being unreasonable. After all, he was only trying to protect me.*

Though her vision was still blurred, her thoughts grew crystal clear. Shaking her head, she said, "No. *No!* I'm not blaming myself for this!" Bounding up from the desk, she stomped out of the storage building, mumbling through clenched teeth, "You walked out on *me*, Mr. Neal-Petty-Officer-Crowson! And you'd better be at that game tomorrow, or else!"

Or else what? She didn't quite know. But one thing she knew for sure—she would be there, ready for action, and dressed to kill. *And*, she told herself, *if he's not standing on that baseball field at game time, he'd better hope the Secret Service catches him before I do!*

Katherine stewed all evening, pacing, then sitting, then pacing again. She knew she was right, but Neal was so stubborn! *Let him get caught*, she told herself. *It would serve him right!* She walked to the bed and sat down in defiance, back straight, chin up, and arms crossed at her breast. But she knew she couldn't stand by and let him self-destruct. She had to do something.

But what? She'd been here before but came up with no plausible plan. It seemed impossible. How could Neal be exonerated? Why would they believe his side of the story? He had no alibi. He'd been on the run. And if he was innocent, why hadn't he come forward, to begin with? Katherine knew the punishment for being AWOL wasn't terribly bad. But the murder charge...the sentence for murder could be terminal. That *had* to be what caused him to run.

She slouched over in defeat, exhausted at not being able to create a feasible plan. But surrendering to defeat had a strange, calming effect. Places, faces, and thoughts began to flash in her mind, playing over and over like a cinematic reel in a 'loop' mode.

The stadium, Father, Neal, AWOL, the ship, murder, home,

Agent Clay, Dr. Akers, the clinic…. Father, Neal, Navy, Agent Clay, Dr. Akers, the clinic…. Neal, Agent Clay, Dr. Akers, the clinic….

"That's it!" she said aloud. Neal, Agent Clay, Dr. Akers, the clinic! Through gritted teeth, she scowled, "The dastardly-doctor-coroner *will* help me get Neal out of the stadium. And the honorable Agent Clay can bend the mind of the Navy sargent at arms…I hope!"

Katherine left her room and crept down the stairs to the foyer hall. She listened intently for evidence of her father in his study, her mother in the parlor, or Subie in the kitchen. Satisfied that no one was within hearing distance, she lifted the phone receiver from the cradle arm and turned the crank handle just enough to alert the operator.

It only took a few seconds for the operator to answer, "Switchboard."

"Houston Secret Service Office, please."

"Yes, ma'am. What is your authorization code?"

"Excuse me?"

"An authorization code is required to connect you to that number, ma'am. Do you have an authorization code?"

"No, I—look, this is an emergency. I need you to connect me immediately. It's a matter of national security!"

"I'm sorry, ma'am. I'm required to get—"

"*Listen to me!*" Katherine interrupted. She detested name-dropping but felt it was her only option. "I am Katherine Bailey, daughter of Senator Joseph Bailey, who is a close friend of Texas Governor Thomas Campbell, President Theodore

Roosevelt, and Theodore Newton Vail, your boss. I strongly suggest you place this call immediately, or I will report you and hold you personally responsible for the consequences!"

"Yes, Miss Bailey, I apologize. I'm connecting you now."

Katherine regretted her tone with the operator. But before she had time to berate herself too brutally, she heard the rude, blunt greeting of what sounded like an agitated male. "Yes?"

She gulped before answering, "Agent Clay, please."

"Who's calling?"

"Katherine Bailey."

"Well, hello, Katherine," the tone instantly changed. "It is indeed a pleasure to hear your voice. What can I do for you?"

She immediately recognized the more professional voice of the agent. "Agent Clay, do you have any influence with the Department of the Navy?"

"Well, now," he said with a chuckle, "you certainly get straight to the point!"

Katherine was not amused. "Well, do you?"

Agent Clay sensed her mood and shifted to a more serious demeanor. "Miss Katherine, the Secret Service operates for and communicates regularly with the office of the president. From that perspective, I'm sure we would have some influence with any department of the federal government." Knowing where her question was leading, he added, "But the Navy won't exonerate a murder suspect without reasonable evidence."

"What if that exoneration was in exchange for incriminating

evidence against a criminal of more imminent importance to the Secret Service and to the economic security of our nation?"

There was a moment of quiet on the receiver. Agent Clay responded, "You have my attention, Miss Bailey."

She knew she had played her cards right, had piqued his interest. "I have a plan that would facilitate your justifiable apprehension of Dr. George Akers. But you must promise me, guarantee me, that you'll do everything within your power to free Neal."

"I don't know what I can do, but—"

"*Promise me!*"

"Okay. I promise to do everything I can to see that he is given fair treatment; that his testimony will be given unbiased credence. But that's all I can do."

"That's all I ask."

Agent Clay added, "And that is provided that your evidence or plan has any merit."

"Oh, I can assure you, it does," Katherine said.

"Yes, well, I'll be the judge of that." Katherine was offended by his remark but held her tongue as he continued, "So, I'm interested to hear this plan of yours. Go ahead; I'm all ears."

"I can't talk here. Can you meet me tomorrow morning at Sam's Café on Brazos Street, 9 a.m.?"

"Sam's Café, Brazos Street. I wouldn't miss it for the world."

Chapter 20: Date to the Game

The cathedral top phone on the wall at the base of the stairway rang out the familiar code for the senator's line. *Rrriiinnnggg-ring-rrriiinnnggg! Rrriiinnnggg-ring-rrriiinnnggg!* Katherine had just returned home from her meeting with Agent Clay on Brazos Street and was about to ascend the stairs to her room. She picked up the receiver. "Hello?"

"Hello, is this Miss Katherine?"

"Yes, it is."

"I wasn't expecting you to be home yet."

She recognized Agent Clay's voice. "Benjamin is excellent with the Ford. And he knows all the shortcuts."

"I'm sure," he dismissed. Katherine felt certain he considered humor a wasted emotion. "Is your father home?"

"Yes. One moment, please." She set the earpiece on the hall table under the phone.

She knocked on the library door and opened it enough to peek in. "Father?"

"Yes?"

Trying to maintain the appearance of her dislike for the man, she continued in a satirical tone, "The wonderful, highly respected, and above-all-reproach Agent Clay would like to speak with you on the phone."

"Now, Katherine, he's just doing his job."

"Yes, well, let him do it by himself! You don't have to help him!"

The senator glanced at her with a condemnable smirk as he walked to his desk and picked up the library extension. "Hang up the phone in the hall…please."

Katherine turned and walked out of the library, closing the door behind her. She picked up the earpiece, and just as she was about to hang it up, she stopped. She placed her right palm over the mouthpiece and, with her left hand in one quick, fluid motion, moved the earpiece receiver down and back up. She put the earpiece to her ear.

"Agent Clay, what can I do for you?"

"Hello, senator. I just have a couple of quick things for you."

"Okay."

"Do you know for certain that Dr. Akers will be at the game today?"

"Well, I feel quite sure that he will. We haven't discussed it, but he usually goes to all the home games. And this being the championship, I can't see him missing it."

"In all due respect, sir, feeling 'quite sure' means you aren't certain."

"Well, I—"

"Are you going to the game?"

"Yes, I am. Considering your comment about having 'both rabbits in the same cage,' I thought it might be interesting to see what happens."

"Okay. Here's what I need you to do. Call Dr. Akers and tell him you'd like to sit with him at the game."

"I can do that."

"Do that now—I need you to do that now. And call me right back and let me know what he says."

"I'll talk to you in a few minutes." Senator Bailey hung up the phone, and Katherine did as well.

The action and information both frightened and excited her. She wanted to hear her father's conversation with Dr. George, but she knew she couldn't be on the phone when the senator was placing a call. And if she picked up during the call, he was certain to hear that telltale click. The only thing to do was listen at the library door.

"Good morning, George," she heard her father say. "Good, good, thank you. I'm thinking about going to the big game today. You going to be there?" The senator was quiet for a moment, then laughed, probably from some comment from Dr. George that she doubted was as amusing as Father made it out to be. From that moment, most of the conversation was a string of mumbles and an occasional laugh. Her father was *laying it on thick*, she thought. The senator's tone was pleasant, but she was glad the conversation was short. Then she heard the answer she was waiting on. "Sounds good, George. I'll see you at 1:45 p.m. Goodbye."

Katherine sped away and hid behind the staircase just in case Father came out before placing the call to Agent Clay. She knew him well; he stepped out of the library door and glanced around the entry hall. Then, seeing no one, he went back in, closing the door behind him. Katherine's mind raced. She desperately wanted to hear her father's conversation with Agent Clay, but listening at the door would only give her one side of the conversation.

Then an idea struck her. She took a small piece of paper from the bookshelf underneath the stairway and folded it several times. When she thought it was about the right size, she snuck over to the phone in the hall. She lifted the earpiece off the receiver and heard her father instructing the operator to place the call.

"Hold on, operator. I think someone just picked up." Katherine forced the small paper wad under the receiver to hold it in the up position, then placed the earpiece back on the receiver. As the library door was opening, she darted back to her hiding place behind the staircase.

Senator Bailey stepped into the hall and glanced over at the phone to see if anyone was there. But there was no one, and the earpiece was hung on the receiver as it should be. He stood for a moment, then went back into the library.

Katherine slipped back to the phone, picked up the earpiece, and put it to her ear. She heard the ring on the other end of the line; once, twice, then someone picked up.

"Yes?"

"Agent Clay, please."

"This is Clay, senator."

"It's set, sir. Dr. George is saving me a seat. I'm to meet him at 1:45 p.m."

"Good. Now, if you see me at the stadium, ignore me. You don't know me; you have never met me. I'm just another fan. Got it?"

"Got it."

"At some point, there will be some action, so just sit tight. At the appropriate time, I'll send for you."

"Send for me?"

"That's all you need to know. Oh! Make sure Miss Katherine attends the game."

"I haven't asked her if she's going."

"Take her. Have her sit in the middle, between you and Dr. Akers."

"Got it."

Katherine waited until Agent Clay and the senator were both off the line. She pulled the paper wad from under the receiver, then hung up the earpiece and darted off to the kitchen. As she pulled a cup from the cabinet, she heard her father come out of the library.

"Katherine?" he called up the stairs.

"In the kitchen, Father." She filled the cup with water and stood at the sink, taking a sip as her father entered the room.

He entered with a confident smile, trying to make conversation. "The man who invented water knew what he was doing!"

Katherine rolled her eyes. "Spare me, Father. What did the hangman want?"

"Katherine!" he scolded. "Agent Clay is just trying to do his job. At least give him credit for being good at it." Katherine just stared at him, waiting for an answer. "He was just being friendly, asked me if I was going to the game. And that gave me an idea; why don't you go with me? You haven't been to a game this year, and this is the championship! How often can you see the Buffs play for the championship? Especially," he added with emphasis, "with someone *we know* on the team?"

Katherine paused, never moving her blank stare from her father. Then she replied, "I was planning to go anyway, by myself."

"Well, now you can go with me!" he blurted. "No need for you to go by yourself if I'm going anyway. We'll take the Ford, just you and me. How about it?"

Katherine couldn't help but be amused at her father's efforts to persuade her. Trying to hide a grin, she said, "I suppose that would be tolerable."

"Great!" he cheered as he pumped his fist. "I'll have Benjamin bring the Ford around at 1:15 p.m. Don't be late!"

"Don't *you* be late, or I'll have Benjamin drive me without you."

Chapter 21: Game Day

Sunrise at West End Park was peaceful and serene and blanketed with the wet kiss of the morning dew. The trailing edge of the rising sun had barely cleared the horizon when the tranquility at the park was shattered by preparations for the championship game. Supervisors barked orders at the grounds crew and maintenance men; concession workers stocked shelves with food and drinks. Souvenir vendors set up tables and booths for the fans, and the neighborhood dogs barked at all the unfamiliar and excessive activity. The noise of the pandemonium reverberated around the stadium, growing into a loud cacophony of sound that echoed throughout the clubhouse, waking Neal from the little sleep he was able to get after his conflict with Katherine.

He rubbed his eyes, then stretched stiffly to smooth out the wrinkles of both muscle and mind. He forced himself to a sitting position on the cot. As he sat there, he began to rehash the events of the night before. But it was a short exercise. He knew Katherine was right, and down deep, he knew it all along. His only real option was to get this over with, to clear his name, if possible. It was his only hope for ending this nightmare. Her words echoed in his mind, *whatever happens, happens.* Being honest would at least give him a chance. Being a fugitive would be a lifetime sentence. Whatever the outcome, at least he would have closure and a clear conscience.

So that was his decision. Play the game, then see what happens. Somehow that gave him peace. But then, most decisions do when you choose to do what's right. He'd been taught that all his life. Neal breathed deeply, and as he exhaled, he felt his whole outlook change. He was calm and relaxed, and his mental quietude lifted his spirits. He dressed and then walked out onto the field to enjoy the action and excitement of game-day preparations.

The field was immaculate. Several of the grounds crew guys were walking the field, clearing it of any debris or trash, even clipping newly sprouted seed pods growing up out of the grass. Maintenance was cleaning the dugouts, walkways, and concession areas under the stadium. Neal strolled over to the home plate. He looked up into the stadium seats over third base. It was busy with teenage boys, evidently hired just for this day, picking up any trash they may find and wiping the morning dew off the seats and benches. He gazed into the seats behind the backstop and then to the seats over first base. They were all busy with teenage boys, with teenage energy, chatting and laughing as they quickly swabbed the stadium.

"You ready?" The voice came from his left.

Neal turned to see Coach Hill approaching. "You know," he replied, pointing a finger in the air with one hand, the other hand on his hip, "I was thinking about sitting this one out. It's been a long time since I just sat and watched a game."

"Ho, ho! No chance, Ace! I plan to get my money's worth out of you today!"

Neal laughed. "I'll do my best, coach."

"I know you will," Coach Hill replied.

After a short pause, Neal said, "Coach, no matter what happens today, I want to thank you for giving me this opportunity." He looked all around, taking in the sounds, sights, and smells of the stadium. "I never imagined I'd end up here, in this game." Looking back at Coach Hill, he said, "Thank you for trusting me."

"My pleasure. I believe today is gonna be a really memorable day for the Buffalos fans."

"It could definitely be that, yes, sir!" Neal said, nodding his head. *If you only knew*, he thought.

Coach Hill swatted Neal on the shoulder. "There's some grub on a table by the main gate. Go eat."

"Yes, sir." Neal jogged off toward the main gate.

"And get some rest!"

Neal threw a hand up and waved in response.

...

Blue sky and green grass greeted the fans at West End Park. The air in the stadium was charged with anticipation, and the aroma of hot dogs and cotton candy was intoxicating. Neal left the locker room and walked to the field access door. He opened the door and was met with the hubbub of more excited fans than he'd ever seen gathered in one place. He was mesmerized.

"What do you think?"

Neal turned to see Charlie peering out over his shoulder.

Turning his gaze back to the crowd, he responded, "Wow! I've been in a lot of big games, but never one with a crowd like this."

"Ha, ha!" Charlie laughed. "It's just another game."

Neal stood at the doorway and scanned the crowd. "It's an hour before the game, and the seats from first base all the way around to third are loosely full already!"

Charlie nodded his head. "Wait 'til game time. There'll be a fan in all *two thousand five hundred* seats."

Neal shook his head in awe. "Whew!" Wide-eyed, he scanned the crowd.

"Well," Charlie said, "after a few years of playing in front of crowds like this, there are a few things I know." Pointing toward the outfield, he continued, "That fence out there? Same place as it was yesterday; no closer, no farther out. The ball is the same size, weighs the same, flies the same. And your bat?" He smiled with a confident nod of his head, "It's the very same one you use in every other game."

Neal shifted his gaze from the crowd to Charlie. He stood there in silence, processing the message. Charlie could see the understanding sweep across Neal's expression. Wearing that quick smile of his, he repeated his earlier observation, "It's just another game, James. More fans, same game."

As the rest of the players approached them at the doorway, a broad smile crossed Neal's face. Charlie slapped him on the shoulder and said, "Let's go warm up!" They exited the doorway, and the home crowd cheered as the team ran onto the field.

After a short warm-up, Neal took his place in center field

to shag balls during their brief batting practice. The outfield fence was lined with fans scattered about between both foul poles, apparently standing on some structure on the back side. All that was visible was their heads sticking up above the wall. He could hear the banter of those nearest him, and more than a little of their conversation was about him.

"That's that new guy, James Landis. They say he can catch any fly ball in the outfield, no matter where it goes."

"I hear he can throw the ball from the center-field wall all the way to home plate! And hit a ball clean across Louisiana Street!"

Neal chuckled under his breath. *Across Louisiana Street! Ha! Maybe with a cannon!*

He couldn't help but be flattered by the apparent fame he had garnered in just a few weeks, but he knew he had to ignore any more comments from the bystanders. He quickly refocused, committing his mind and attention back to the practice at hand. After catching a few more balls, Coach Hill called everyone in.

As he neared the dugout, he heard someone in the low seats shout, "Neal!" His head jerked as if he had a tic, but he caught himself before turning full-faced to the stands. Then he heard it again, "Neal! Mr. Baseball!"

Mr. Baseball? He knew it had to be someone from home, or at least someone in his regional Louisiana League. His cover was about to be blown. His heart began to race, and his face felt hot. *Get control of yourself, Neal! You knew you could be recognized, and I guess now is as good a time as later!*

As he took his last few steps to the dugout, he heard voices responding to the caller. "His name ain't Neal."

Another voice rang out, "That's James Landis, the new player. The Buffs picked him up just a few games before the playoffs."

And another, "And it was a good move, I'd say!"

Neal entered the dugout and sat on the bench, shutting out everything around him, mentally withdrawing from his surroundings. He took a deep breath and exhaled, then a deeper breath, and exhaled. *Okay*, he told himself, *you said you wanted to get this over. So let it happen, naturally. You don't have to force it, just let it unfold on its own. Play the game.*

Neal lifted his glove to his nostrils, closed his eyes, and inhaled the familiar, soothing smell of leather. He began to calm down, to feel the anxiety ease away; not completely, but at least enough to be manageable. Gradually, the murmur of his teammates became audible, and their chatter lifted his spirits. The crowd noise returned, as did the scent of fresh popcorn wafting through the dugout. He was back in the moment and glad of it. This was a moment he'd always dreamed of, and he wasn't going to waste it. His determination soared, and his gift of self-motivation kicked in. *Today may be your last game, Neal. Make it your best game ever!*

His resolve was solid. But he couldn't help but wonder who was in the stands. Who was it that called his name? Family? Friend? Enemy? He would have to find out, but he would have to be discreet in his method.

. . .

It was game time, and the Buffalos had home-field

advantage. Neal trotted out to center field, careful not to look up into the stands or acknowledge any voices calling after him. He decided that his opportunity to locate the caller would have to be taken at the end of the inning or maybe a later inning. It would have to be done well before he got too close to the stands, far enough out that he could scan the area visually but keep his head fixed straight ahead. That's it. That was his plan.

The top of the first inning passed quickly; three up, three down. The Buffs trotted in to start their first at bat. On his way in from centerfield, Neal's mind was possessed by the voice in the crowd; he had to find out who had called his name. Just before he entered the dugout, he glanced into the crowd and saw a familiar face. It was Veldon Maxwell, agent for the Shreveport Pirates. It had never dawned on him that Mr. Maxwell would be there, although the possibility should have been obvious.

He entered the dugout and sat on the bench, shutting out the din of the massive crowd, angered at himself for not thinking about Mr. Maxwell, that he could possibly be there. For that matter, he surmised, it was feasible that other scouts and coaches could be there, some who had probably scouted him themselves or had been at games where he had played.

Again, he took a deep breath and exhaled slowly. He knew there was nothing he could do. The task at hand was the game; the rest was out of his control. *"C'est la vie," he said to himself. Such is life.*

"James!" Neal looked up and saw a man who appeared to be from the maintenance crew. He was holding up a piece of paper and motioning for Neal to come over. "Have a note for you," he said with a smile, "from a pretty lady in the

bleachers."

Neal was confused. "Thank you," he said. He walked back to the dugout and went to the end of the bench. He opened it and noticed immediately that it was written by a woman's hand. It was a short three-sentence message: "I'm sitting in the stands behind home plate, slightly to the first base side, with Father and Dr. George. Agent Clay and many other agents are scattered throughout the stands. Play the game."

Neal folded the note and stuffed it in his back pocket, the only pockets on his uniform. Containing his excitement, he took a casual step to the front of the dugout, hung his fingers in the fence, and studied the stands. His heart leaped when he spotted her, right where she said she would be. Sitting on her left and right were the senator and Dr. George. He hoped to make eye contact with her, but she had no idea he was looking and no clue when or if he would get her note. After a few moments gazing at Katherine, Neal looked around the stands. And here and there, he spotted them—black suits, uniformed police, and a couple of Navy officers in white.

Before he knew it, someone shouted, "Let's go!" Neal's attention was snatched back to the game. His teammates were heading back onto the field. The bottom of the inning was the twin of the top; three up, three down.

The top of the second was another shutout. Neal was at bat to start the bottom of the inning. He nailed a fastball, sending it like a meteor into left-center field. It bounced off the wall for a standup double.

Second base is a great vantage point for scanning the stands. He looked behind the backstop and saw Katherine sitting right where she said she would be. Dr. George leaned over her in conversation, apparently trying to entertain the senator with one of his prattling tales. Neal was annoyed but knew Katherine could handle herself if need be. She was a strong and capable woman. He smiled at the thought of Dr. George receiving a dose of her wrath.

He turned his attention back to the game; focusing would help remove the stress of what lies ahead. He stole his way to third before the inning was over.

The Indians scored on a sacrifice fly in the top of the third. The Buffalos were held scoreless.

In the bottom of the fourth, the Buffalos scored on a sacrifice fly by Neal. The inning ended with a score of 1–1. The following four innings were sleepers. There were random hits and walks, but neither team scored.

The ninth started with the score still tied 1–1. The top of the lineup was up for the Indians. The first batter drew a walk, which put pressure on the Buffalos. He was fast and eager to steal second. Batter number two struck out. One out, one on first.

The number three batter was strong, and the right fielder was playing him deep. He got a dirty base hit to short right field, a spinning blooper off the end of the bat that died in the grass. The runner at first took off and never slowed down, speeding past second base and digging his way to third. The right fielder had no choice but to relay the ball to the second baseman. The runner kicked up a cloud of dust as he slid safely into third base.

Next up was the cleanup hitter, known for his explosive hits to the wall and beyond. A base hit could score the go-ahead run, maybe more. Today he was 0 for 2 with a walk, but his batting average was one of the league's highest. The Buffs had to be especially careful here.

Coach Hill didn't know if he was weak at any specific pitch, so he was forced to guess at a pitching strategy. After a couple of low outside pitches, the Buffs pitcher delivered one belt-high over the inside edge of the plate. The batter crushed it, a line drive straight to the third baseman who barely got his glove in front of it before it smashed into his chest. Out number two! The runners remained at first and third!

Again, the situation was dire; two out, two on. The Buffs had to get this batter out, or they'd be in a deep hole. The batter was number five in the line-up. He was a known long-ball hitter but had a mediocre batting average and, so far, no hits in the game. The first pitch was a mistake; belt high and right down the middle, right in the batter's wheelhouse. He drove it deep into center field. Neal was off and running, tracking the ball that was flying directly over his head. At the last moment, he used the wall as a springboard and launched himself high into the air. With his arm stretched high over the wall, the ball landed securely in his glove for out number three.

Neal trotted in from center field. As he crossed the infield, he glanced into the stands and saw law officers standing at every gate around the field. Oddly, he didn't see the Navy officers and black suits, including Agent Clay. He looked up behind home plate to get some sort of reassurance from Katherine. But she was also gone! *Maybe she went to get concessions*, Neal told himself, *or gone to the restroom.*

Glancing back again, he noticed that Dr. George was gone as well. "Strange," he said aloud as he entered the dugout.

"What's strange?" Pat said as Neal passed by.

"Oh, n—nothing. Just talking to myself."

Coach Hill chimed in, "Talk for all of us if you think it'll help. We need some runs." He added, "My bride has plans for me after this game, and she doesn't like extra innings!"

Neal smiled at the quip but couldn't help but be nervous. It was all coming down on him; the game, the feds, the future, Katherine. He knew he was doing the right thing, but knowing it was the easy part. The reality of it was unsettling. *Focus*, he told himself. *Focus!*

It was the bottom of the ninth. The right fielder, Pat Newnam, was up to bat. He was the number three batter, which meant Neal was on deck.

Pat stepped into the batter's box. Neal yelled, "Let's go, Pat! Give us a runner!"

The first pitch was in for a strike, catching Pat on his heels. He dug in, taking a couple of warm-up swings as if he were ready now. The second pitch was low and inside. The count was one and one. The third pitch was an off-speed pitch; Pat swung and missed. It was a nasty curve, starting right down the middle and curving out of reach to the outside of the plate.

"James! James Landis!" Neal heard the voice but chose to ignore it and keep his focus on the game. But the next call caught him by surprise, "Neal!" Before he could restrain himself, he turned to see who was calling. The man behind the backstop fence waving a note at him was Veldon Maxwell, scout for the Shreveport Pirates.

Neal hesitated. Mr. Maxwell waved the note at him again, and with urgency, used both hands to beckon him over. His actions indicated that the note must be important. Over his shoulder, Neal shouted, "Settle down, Pat! Let's go!" Then he jogged over to Mr. Maxwell, who quickly shoved the note through the fence.

As Neal took the note, Maxwell said, "Katherine said it's extremely important, and she said you must trust her."

Neal glanced up at Maxwell. "How do you know Katherine?"

"She heard me call you by your real name and later asked me how I knew you. I told her I had scouted you in Louisiana. Then she asked me to deliver this note. It seemed very urgent."

"Thank you," Neal said as he unfolded the note.

"Good luck!"

Pat stepped back into the batter's box and readied himself for the fourth pitch. With the count one ball and two strikes, he knew the Indian's pitcher, Tom Martin, had the edge. Pat lined up in the back of the box and crowded the plate. Martin delivered a blazing fastball, but it was low and bounced off the plate. The count was two and two.

Martin straddled the rubber and looked to the dugout, waiting for the coach to give the pitch signal. He got it, took a big windup, then threw another curveball. This time it was a bit too far to the outside. The umpire called, "Three and two. Full count!"

Pat stood just outside of the batter's box, wiping his palms one at a time on the thigh of his pants. He knew he had to calm down and get the bat on the ball, somehow, someway. As Martin climbed the hill and settled in for the signal, Pat stepped up to the plate. He planted his back foot in the depression he had dug out for a solid push-off. His front foot he placed below his front shoulder. But he was anything but calm.

He could feel every eye in the stadium focused on him, relishing the familiar battle between pitcher and batter. He knew that some were cheering him on, and some were praying for his demise. He could be the first out of the ninth, possibly saving the Indians for another inning, or he could be the base runner needed to secure a Buffalos win. His palms were already sweaty again.

The seconds raced by, and the pitch call was made. Pat loaded for the pitch, ready to hit whatever came at him. Then came the wind-up, then the delivery. It was another nasty curveball, and Pat couldn't help himself. He swung with all his might—and missed the ball completely. The momentum of his swing caused him to stumble onto one knee.

"Out!" shouted the umpire.

The crowd exploded, mingling bliss and agony in a discordant roar. Pat was numb and deaf with disappointment. He stood, nodded at Martin, then turned and plodded toward the dugout. As he approached Neal, he murmured in defeat, "I was looking for a fastball."

Neal patted him on the back as he passed, though he wasn't even sure what the pitch had been. He had been too consumed by the contents of Katherine's note, the contents of which seemed inconceivable. "You must trust me," she said. "Play the game." It all seemed crazy to Neal, but in this situation, he felt he had no other choice.

But right now, the task at hand was getting a hit. He knew this might be the last at bat of his short career, so he had to make it count. The intensity of that realization heightened each of his senses. With his bat on his shoulder, he stopped and took a deep breath, absorbing every detail of the moment in a single instant. He relished the noise of the crowd, cheering and screaming and jumping and waving in un-orchestrated revelry. Despite the summer heat, their excitement and energy raised goosebumps on his arms. The sun beamed down through a beautiful cloud-free sky, glinting off glass pains, painted surfaces, and bright colored hatpins. He savored the mixed aromas of concessions, leather, and fresh cut grass.

It was his time, and he knew what he must do. He was resolved to his fate. As he and Katherine had agreed, this was the best thing, the only path to closure and freedom. He must place his trust in the authorities and tell his side of the story. The truth. Then his duty would be done and his conscious clear. Truth is freedom, and a clear conscience is peace. The rest was out of his hands.

With that thought, Neal took a deep breath, then recommitted his resolve. In a faint whisper, he repeated Katherine's words that had become his strength. "Whatever happens, happens. Play the game."

He took another deep breath, then blew it out. *Okay, Neal,* he thought. *Do your job.* Abruptly, he turned toward the crowd behind the backstop and searched for Katherine. She was back! He felt immediate relief. Catching his gaze, she sat upright stared at him, giving him her undivided attention. Even in the stress of the moment, the first thought Neal had when he saw her was how beautiful she was. He smiled. She always made him smile.

He raised his eyebrows and pursed his lips as if to say *this is it*. Katherine pressed her hands together and raised them to her lips, partially obscuring her nervous smile. She held Neal with her eyes, and for an instant, he was oblivious to the world.

"James!" Still gazing at Katherine, the name didn't register.

"James!" The voice, suddenly at his shoulder, startled him. He flinched and glanced around quickly to see Coach Hill at his side.

"Settle down, Ace! You'll see her after the game," the coach teased. Neal smiled, somewhat embarrassed. Coach continued, "Look. This is just another at bat. Since you've been on this team, you've hit every pitcher you've faced. And you've faced some of the top guys in the league." Coach nodded toward Martin on the mound, "This chump is not as good as some you've already knocked the socks off of. He's only here because he has a great defense backing him up. Got it?"

"Yes, sir!" Neal smiled, then added, "But he *does* have a good fastball."

"And a nasty curve!" coach laughed. "Look, you hit faster pitches the first day you practiced with us. Now, get up there and crush it!"

Neal nodded and strode toward the plate. It was a short walk, but in those few steps, he was able to tune out all the distractions, those very sights, smells, and emotions that he had relished just a few seconds earlier. His focus was now on the challenge at hand: pitcher against batter, batter against pitcher. It was a challenge he loved and one he seldom lost.

Neal stepped into the batter's box and kicked dirt in the foot hole at the rear of the box. He likes a push-off spot for his back foot, but a lot of the players dig a foot hole that a rabbit could get lost in. He never saw the point in that. He filled the hole to the top, then packed the dirt with his foot to make it firm. Then he scratched a little out of it with his cleats, just enough to get the angle he liked. He settled into position, first the back foot and then the front. As was his habit, he leaned over and tapped the outside of the plate twice, stood up straight, and rested the bat on his shoulder.

Martin stood ready on the mound. He took the call from the pitching coach, nodded his head, and placed his foot on the rubber. Neal loosened his muscles one last time, circling his bat through the zone a time or two. Then he readied the bat, hands gripping the handle just a few inches off his shoulder, bat head extending backward and angled up toward the top seats of the grandstands. He crouched just enough to equalize the tension between upper body and lower, melding them into one powerful mass of potential energy.

Martin stared at the mitt. He picked his spot for the pitch and began his wind-up. Being tall and slender exaggerated his unusual delivery. *Probably why he's effective*, Neal thought as he studied the antics. Somehow, he lifted his front foot nearly as high as his head, and his pitching arm was dropped so far back the ball almost dragged in the dirt. From this contorted position, he whipped forward in a sudden jerk, sending a fastball whizzing just off the plate and waking Neal from his musing.

Pushing the palm of his hand to the right, the umpire yelled, "Outside! Ball one!"

Neal was glad the pitch was a ball but was surprised Martin would go to the outside. All the scouting reports showed that Neal could crush a pitch over the outside half of the plate, so he was expecting an inside pitch.

He stepped away from the plate to collect his thoughts. He took a deep breath, then with a slight shake of his head, blew it out. *Focus, Neal. Focus!*

Martin was back on the mound. Neal stepped into the box,

tapped his bat on the plate, and got set for the pitch. Martin, again with his exaggerated style, let it fly. It was another fastball, up and inside, just as Neal had expected. He let it pass for strike one.

Never stepping out of the box, he tapped the plate as usual. As he pulled his bat up to the ready position, the ball whizzed by. Martin had delivered a quick pitch.

"Strike two!" called the umpire.

Neal stepped out of the batter's box and threw a gaze of protest at the umpire.

Pointing down at Neal's feet, he replied, "You were in the box."

The catcher laughed. "Caught you on your heels, didn't he?" he goaded. "Gotta pay attention, boy; stay on your toes!"

Neal paused to let it all sink in. First two fastballs, then the quick pitch, then the sarcasm. He knew they were trying to get into his head. In an instant, his demeanor changed from anger to determination, and a smile crossed his lips. He nodded at the catcher and said, "Okay." He placed one foot in the batter's box and tapped the plate. With his eyes studying Martin, he moved the other foot into position and circled his bat through the zone. He was set.

Martin threw a curveball that started off down the middle. Neal loaded up to swing but stopped short as he caught the faint curve starting to develop. It continued to curve and crossed the plate low and outside.

"Two and two!" shouted the umpire.

"Oooh, almost went for it!" said the catcher. "Just go

ahead, take the next strike, get it over with. I need to stand up and stretch a bit."

Neal grinned. "I'll see if I can help you with that."

"Yeah, you do that. I love to stretch while you guys trot back to the dugout."

Neal chuckled. As he stepped back into the batter's box, it occurred to him that Martin had a less exaggerated windup when he threw the curveball. Maybe he could use that to his advantage.

Martin was on the mound arguing pitch calls from the coach. After a couple of shake-offs, they finally reached an agreement. Martin placed his foot on the rubber and got set for the pitch. He made his move, and the delivery motion was the same as the last. Neal watched as the ball curved outside and into the dirt.

Without a word, the umpire threw both of his hands to the outside of the plate to indicate a wide pitch. Then holding both fists over his head, he yelled, "Full count!"

Neal stepped out of the box. Three balls, two strikes. He knew he had to make contact if the next pitch was good. But he also knew the pressure was really on Martin. If Martin threw a ball, Neal would get a walk to first. If he threw a strike, Neal would have the chance to get a base hit, maybe multiple bases, or even crush it for a homer. If nothing else, he could foul it off and force Martin to throw another strike, giving himself all the same options a second time.

Neal stepped to the edge of the batter's box and looked toward the mound. Apparently, Martin and his coach agreed on the pitch; Martin was already standing on the rubber.

Guarding against another quick pitch, Neal locked his gaze on Martin. He moved his back foot into place in the batter's box, then eased his front foot into position. Still staring at Martin, he tapped the plate with his bat and circled the bat through the zone, slowly, deliberately. He was ready for business.

Martin took a wide stance, staring hard into the catcher's mitt. Then, as he stood upright to set for the pitch, he shifted his gaze to Neal. Without hesitation, Neal did something unusual, something that had worked for him in the past. He blew a kiss at Martin.

Martin's haunting, sarcastic eyes changed to demonic, glaring with rage. And that was his mistake. He started his pitching motion, reaching way back to the dirt. Neal recognized the windup and loaded for the fastball. Martin whipped the pitch with every ounce of strength in his body. Neal was right. It was a blazing fastball, just under belt high and over the outside half of the plate. Right in Neal's wheelhouse.

Neal exploded on the pitch. He heard the loud *crack* of the impact but felt no resistance. He knew it was well hit, right in the sweet spot. He took off to first base, watching the ball sail out toward left-center field. It continued to rise as if it had grown wings, taking its sweet time before arcing over the heads of the running outfielders. They slowed to a stop, knowing there was no chance for a play, and stood and watched as the ball disappeared behind the wall.

The home crowd went wild, cheering and screaming at the top of their lungs. The grandstands sprang to life as fans jumped and spun, waving and flailing their arms in the air. The umpire circled his hand high over his head, the league signal for a home run. Then he turned to the catcher and, over the din of the crowd, said, "Got your wish. Start stretchin'."

Neal slowed his pace and trotted around the bases, careful to step squarely on every base as he passed. As he crossed third and headed toward home plate, he gazed into the stands to find Katherine. It only took a moment, although she was surrounded and partially hidden by a hoard of celebrating fans. She stood still, hands clasped in front of her chest, doing her best to smile. Then with a slight tilting of her head, she motioned toward the gates leading onto the field.

He knew what she meant. There were law enforcement officers at every entrance. His cheering teammates and coaches surrounded him as he jogged the last few steps toward home, where he leaped into the air and landed with both feet squarely on home plate. His excited teammates closed in, knocking him to the ground and piling on top in a huge dogpile.

Closing in fast were suits and uniforms pushing and shoving their way through the emotional players from both teams. Some were making their way directly to the mass of players piled on the ground, and others were merely present for crowd control. The authorities rushed forward and began to disburse all who were not members of the Buffalos ballclub. Others assisted the coaches and began to pull and drag players from the pile. Players from the lower levels of the pile were under tremendous weight and pressure, many coming out with injuries, gasping for air, moaning, and coughing.

Finally, the last player was pulled off Neal. He remained on the ground, face down, motionless. Coach Hill carefully rolled Neal onto his side. Neal remained lifeless.

Coach shouted, "Call for the doc! Somebody, call for the doc!"

"Calm down! The doc is here!"

Coach Hill looked up and immediately recognized one of the Buffalos' leading benefactors, Dr. George Akers. Alarmed, the coach said, "He doesn't seem to be breathing, Dr. George."

"Stand back; let me look at him." He looked around and addressed the hovering crowd, "Everybody, get back and give him some room!" Law enforcement officials stepped in and began to move the spectators away from the scene, urging them to disperse and go home. Most moved away, but few left.

Dr. Akers got down on one knee and turned Neal onto his back. He gripped Neal's wrist to check for a pulse. But after a few seconds, he shook his head and laid the lifeless hand back on the ground. He put his ear to Neal's chest to listen for a heartbeat but soon sat back up on his knees. He sat still, staring down at the body.

Senator Bailey fought against the receding crowd. As he emerged from the group, Katherine darted around him and ran forward, pushing her way through Secret Service agents and Navy personnel. She plopped onto her knees at Neal's side and clasped his unresponsive hand. "Dr. George, is he alright? Will he be okay?"

Dr. Akers looked over at her. With a slight shake of his head, he said, "I'm sorry, Katherine."

"No!" she cried. Shaking Neal's hand, she yelled, "Neal! Neal!" Dr. George placed his hand on her shoulder. She jerked away, screaming, "Do something! Do something, Dr. George! You've got to do something!"

"Katherine, it's too late," he replied.

She pressed his hand to her face and sobbed in anguish.

Tears flowed down her delicate cheek and pooled between his thumb and forefinger, then coursed over the back of his hand and dripped onto the thick dust of the batter's circle. Senator Bailey stooped down and put his arms around her, consoling in silence as best he could.

Dr. George looked back and extended a hand to someone standing behind him. It was Agent Clay, who quickly stepped up and helped Dr. George to his feet. They stepped away from the scene, and Agent Clay asked, "What happened, Dr. Akers?"

Again, Dr. Akers shook his head before replying. "Pile-ups are agony for those on the bottom."

"Yes, but generally, people survive it. What happened here?"

"It appears he was face down in the dirt. I suppose, in his gasping to breathe, he inhaled a dose of dust and choked under the pile."

With a quick wag of his head, Agent Clay said, "Horrible way to go."

Dr. George turned back to the group surrounding Neal and noticed the unusual attire present. Most of the people in the group were dressed in uniforms. He cocked his head in thought and asked, "Why are there so many law enforcement officials here?"

"Well, the particulars are confidential. I'm Agent Ronald Clay of the Secret Service. This player happens to have some information of particular interest to us and to the Department of the Navy as well."

"I see," Dr. George nodded. "Well, unfortunately for you

folks, he won't be able to answer any questions. And, as I'm the coroner for Houston County, I need to take possession of the body and transport it to the morgue at my clinic. There's a lot of work to be done and not much time to do it."

Agent Clay nodded. "I understand. Oh, Dr. Akers," he added, "the Secret Service and the Navy will both need an official death certificate to close out our case files."

"Absolutely! Since it's urgent, I'll complete the medical examination today. You can send someone by for the certificates tomorrow."

"We'll get them today," Agent Clay replied. "I don't mind waiting." Dr. Akers made no response but was visibly angered.

As they rejoined the group, Agent Clay stopped beside one of the Navy officials. Dr. Akers walked over to Senator Bailey, who was still kneeling beside Katherine, arm around her shoulders. He leaned over and whispered, "Senator, I need to take the body to the morgue."

The senator nodded. He gave Katherine a quick, firm squeeze. "Katherine—"

"I heard him," she muttered. She kissed Neal's hand, then laid it neatly on his chest. With her father's help, she stood to her feet, stared down at Neal for a moment, then turned to Dr. Akers. Nodding toward Neal, she said, "I'm riding with him to the clinic."

"Katherine," Dr. Akers replied, "You don't want to—"

"Don't ever presume to tell me what I want!" she snapped. "I *am* riding with him to the clinic, and that's final! Father, you can ride with us if you like. If not, have Benjamin drop you off wherever you want, then send him to the clinic to pick me up."

"I'll go with you," he replied. "Benjamin can follow us over." Turning to Agent Clay, the senator added, "If it would help, Agent Clay, you could follow my driver, Benjamin, to the morg—to Dr. Akers' clinic."

"That would be good, senator."

"I'll have him meet you at the main entrance. He'll be driving a Ford Model K."

"I'll find him," Agent Clay said. He turned a mumbled something to his assistant, Agent Ben Todd, and the two of them walked over to the Navy officers and began an inaudible conversation.

Dr. Akers leaned in close to the senator. "Tell Benjamin to take his time," he whispered. "Maybe take a somewhat indirect route. I need a bit of time, y—you know, to uh—to get the paperwork in order."

"Agent Clay said he wouldn't mind waiting."

"Please!" Dr. Akers pled. "It's very important that I have a little time."

Katherine interrupted, "It's fine, Father. I wouldn't want the hangman looking over my shoulder either."

"Alright, alright! You two beat all!"

"I'll drive my car to the south gate, senator. I believe that's as close as I can get. Please have some men meet me there with the body.

"You and Katherine can ride with me from there."

"Sounds good."

Chapter 22: The Morgue

The loud banging on the door resonated down the empty halls of the clinic, rolling like thunder in the dark bowels of the morgue.

Struggling to finish his paperwork, Dr. Akers shouted, "My heavens! Let them in before they knock the bloody door down!"

Senator Bailey rushed down the hall to the lobby and yelled through the door, "Hold on, let me unlock it!" He unhooked the chain from the door then turned the large key. The bolt retracted with a loud *click*.

On the other side of the door was Agent Clay. Behind him were Agent Todd, two Navy masters at arms, Chief of Police Ernest West, and one of his officers. "Excuse us, senator," Agent Clay said, "but we knocked for quite some time before we decided to bang on the door."

"Yes. Well, I guess we should have mentioned the back door. It's the entry to the morgue."

"After the indirect route your driver led us on, he could have at least led us to the correct entrance."

"Indirect route? I'm sorry, Agent Clay. I'll have a talk with him about that."

After the group entered, Senator Bailey closed the door behind them and turned the big key. He checked the door to make sure it was secured, then stepped around the men to the open door of the hallway. "Follow me," he said. Then he led the procession down the long, dimly lit hall to the morgue.

Near the end of the hall, he looked back at the group behind him. There were no stragglers. Seasoned professionals as they were, they were all speechless. Silent. Bunched together like children tiptoeing through a haunted house. Under other circumstances, he would have found it amusing. But given the happenings of the day, there was nothing funny about it. It was a dismal, depressing time.

Senator Bailey knocked on the door at the end of the hall. As he turned the knob and pulled the door open, he called, "We have visitors, doc."

"Bring them in. I'm almost finished with these certificates."

The air from the examination room wafted over the group. Several of the men frowned, and some even covered their nose and mouth with a handkerchief or sleeve as they filed into the poorly lit room. Senator Bailey followed Chief West into the room. When he closed the door, the sound bounced around the room as if they were in a cave.

The room had very few furnishings. Here and there were a few wheeled trays with various surgical tools lying on top. Numerous chemicals and medicines were scattered on the open wall shelves. In the middle of the room, under a single bright light, was an examination table covered with a sheet. The profile of a body was obvious. As the men spread out around the room, Agent Clay asked, "Why is there such a strong odor of—of chloroform?"

Dr. Akers looked up from his paperwork, "Oh, uh—it—it's a clinic, Agent Clay. What did you expect?"

"I didn't expect chloroform in a morgue."

"It's a—a multi-purpose examination room," Dr. Akers said. Turning back to his paperwork, he added, "Embalming isn't the only activity that takes place in here."

"Well, I'm not going to ask what else," Agent Clay answered. He stepped over to the examination table and pulled back the sheet just enough to reveal Neal's head. Katherine looked away and pulled her open hand up to her brow, shielding her view of the scene. Staring at the lifeless face, he asked, "What's the official cause of death?" He glanced across the room at Katherine, "Please excuse the bluntness, ma'am." She didn't respond.

"Suffocation, just as I had expected. He had a bit of dirt in his mouth, but there was no sign of choking. So, it's suffocation."

"Suffocation," Agent Clay thought aloud, "under a pile of cheering, celebrating teammates."

"You can bet not all those near the bottom were celebrating," Dr. Akers replied. Tipping his head toward Neal, he added, "Likely they were struggling just as much as he was. I've always said these 'dog piles' are about the most ignorant thing a team can do."

"Yes, I'm sure," said Agent Clay.

Dr. Akers turned and approached Agent Clay. "I know you and these fine Navy officers are short on time, so I completed the death certificates posthaste," he said, waving several sheets of paper in the air to finish drying the ink. "Two for you, and two for the Navy. No need for you to waste your time around here."

"Are you in a rush for us to leave, Dr. Akers?"

"N—No, of course not. I just know you are busy, and—I'm trying to be respectful of your valuable time."

"How thoughtful of you to consider our time." Agent Clay took the death certificates from Dr. Akers, gave two copies to the chief master at arms, and kept the other two copies. He stood by the examination table under the light, reading the entirety of the document. Everyone else in the room stood in silence, waiting for Agent Clay to finish examining the certificate.

Dr. Akers began to fidget. "It's all official, I can assure you."

"Yes, I'm sure." Agent Clay responded as he began to pace slowly. He swung his hands behind his back and grasped his right wrist with his left hand. The death certificates were still clutched between his right thumb and index finger; they stuck out behind his back like a tail on a crowing rooster. "Dr. Akers," he began, "just how do you, as a coroner, determine beyond any doubt that a person is actually deceased?"

"Oh, j—just the usual things."

"Such as?"

"Well, basically, no breathing and no heartbeat for an extended period of time is a dead giveaway." Turning to Katherine, he added, "If you'll excuse the terminology, Miss Katherine. After about fifteen to twenty minutes without oxygen or blood circulation, a body can't survive."

"Yes, that's generally the case," Agent Clay said. "There are always exceptions, of course."

Dr. Akers responded, "Oh, always. Yes."

"Did you use any further observations or methods to ensure his demise?"

"There was no need. He's been without vitals for more than an hour now. No one can survive that."

"True, true," Agent Clay agreed. He moved his left hand from behind his back, rested his fingertips on his chin, and tapped his lips with his forefinger. After a moment in thought, he stopped his pacing and turned toward Dr. Akers. "In recent years, hasn't it been discovered that a corpse has no blood pressure?"

Dr. Akers shifted his stance. "Y—yes, I believe that's true."

"Do you have a sphygmomanometer?"

"Yes."

"You didn't try taking his blood pressure when you got here?"

"No. Again, due to the time lapse, I felt there was no point in it."

"Why don't we take his blood pressure now? You, know, just for the record."

"That would be pointless, sir. It would only be wasting more of your valuable time."

"Let me worry about my time, Dr. Akers. Let's do it, just

for the record."

"Well, actually, Agent Clay, I would be glad to oblige. But my sphygmomanometer has been malfunctioning lately. I sent it out for repairs earlier this week."

"Out for repairs," Agent Clay repeated, nodding his head. "How unfortunate." He began to pace again. As he reached the foot of the corps, he stopped momentarily and spoke to Agent Todd in tones inaudible to anyone else in the group. Then he turned and strolled directly toward Dr. Akers.

"Dr. Akers, does a corpse bleed?"

"That depends. When a corpse lies still, in whatever position it may be, gravity pulls the blood to the lowest points of the body. If a cut or puncture is in any of the lower areas, then, yes, the body will appear to bleed. But it's due to gravity, not an active heart."

"Yes, that's correct," Agent Clay replied. He cast a questioning glance at Agent Todd, who answered with a slight nod of his head. Agent Clay then turned and raised a hand toward Dr. Akers. The other arm he extended toward the foot of the corpse. "Let me show you something, Dr. Akers. Right this way."

As the two men approached, Agent Todd stepped away from the end of the examination table, allowing them plenty of room. Agent Clay positioned Dr. Akers and himself directly at the end of the table, facing the feet of the corpse.

"Dr. Akers, a few moments ago, I asked Agent Todd to do me a favor. You see, I know Agent Todd well enough to know that he always carries a razor-sharp folding blade in his pocket." Dr. Akers' stance stiffened noticeably. "So, while you were explaining the effect that gravity has on the blood of a corpse, Agent Todd discreetly raised the sheets at Neal's feet. And if he followed my instructions correctly, he made a small incision on the little toe of the left foot."

He threw the corner of the sheet onto Neal's shins, exposing the left foot. Blood had trickled down the little toe, run across the ball of the foot, and dripped down to form a small stain on the mattress sheet.

For a few seconds, Dr. Akers stared at the foot. He jerked his gaze up to Agent Clay. "It can take a while. The blood sometimes takes a while to drain down—"

"When does the chloroform wear off?" Agent Clay demanded.

"Th—the blood doesn't always—"

"How long until the chloroform wears off!"

"I don't know what you're talking about!" Dr. Akers skirted around the examination table, backing away from the officials.

Agent Clay shouted, "I'm talking about lying to agents of the Secret Service, aiding and abetting a criminal, falsifying federal documents, white slavery, associating with anarchists, if not an anarchist yourself. And I'm sure my investigation, which will be thorough, will confirm your extensive counterfeiting operation. At the least, Dr. Akers, you're looking at a lifetime in prison!"

Still backing away, Dr. Akers pointed at Katherine. "It's her fault! She blackmailed me!"

"Agreeing to yield to your sexual advances is not

blackmail, Dr. Akers. We call it bait. And the sleazy bottom sucker always gets hooked and landed."

Dr. Akers was outwitted and outnumbered, and he knew it. He began to check his options. There were two ways out of the room; one was the hall door, and the other was the rear access door. His path to the hall door was blocked by the examination table and the Secret Service agents. The police officers and Navy officials were blocking his way to the rear exit door. Katherine sat at the head of the examination table, just behind Dr. Akers. There was no clear path of escape. Panic began to take over, and his fear soon turned to anger and rage.

In desperation, he snatched a scalpel from an instrument tray and, with the other hand, jerked Katherine out of the chair. He stepped behind her and wrapped his left arm around her waist, squeezing her until she found it hard to breathe. He held the scalpel to her throat. "Nobody move!" he said through clenched teeth. "I know the precise position of the carotid artery. One quick slash, and she'll bleed out in seconds."

"George!" Senator Bailey shouted. "That's Katherine you're holding!"

"Yes, it is, senator. And if you want her to remain unharmed, you better make sure these gentlemen do exactly as I say."

The senator turned to Agent Clay. "Please, Agent Clay! Please—do as he says!"

Pumping his open hands in front of his chest, Agent Clay instructed, "Everyone, stay where you are and remain calm. Just remain calm." For a moment, no one spoke. He took a deep breath, then continued, "Dr. Akers, you're only making your situation worse. Let her go. We can talk this out."

"Quiet!" Akers shouted. "I'm doing the talking now. You just listen!" Using the scalpel as a pointer, he said, "Move to the front of the room. Slowly!" As the men made their way to the front of the room, he moved away from the examination table and opposite to their movement.

Dr. Akers backed over to the rear exit door, pulling Katherine with him. "Katherine is going with me," he said with a sneer. "I would strongly suggest, gentlemen, that you stay where you are until the sound of my motorcar fades completely out of earshot. Agent Clay, is that understood?"

"Yes."

"Can I have your word on that?"

"Until it's completely out of earshot. Yes."

"Thank you, sir. You're a wise man. A wise man indeed." Turning to the senator, Dr. Akers adds, "Senator, Agent Clay holds the fate of your daughter in his hands. I trust that you'll make sure he honors his word."

"George, don't do this," the senator pleads. "Please let her go!"

"Senator! Did you hear me?"

Raising his open hands in the air, he responds, "Absolutely, George. He'll honor his word."

"Good. That's very good." The slow, sinister smile of a deranged man spread across his face, and his eyes grew wide in anticipation of escape. "Gentlemen," he said, "it is with great pleasure I bid you *adieu!*" He reached back with his left hand, turned the knob, and pushed the door open. Still holding the scalpel to Katherine's throat, he backed through the open door.

Whack!

The men flinched at the sudden noise. They watched in shock as Dr. Akers' knees buckled and he collapsed to the ground. Katherine shrieked and jumped back into the room, staring down at his limp body in disbelief.

The silhouette of a man darkened the glare of the afternoon sun flooding into the open doorway. "I didn't have no club, Miss Katherine, but this tire wrench sho can make do."

"Benjamin! Father, it's Benjamin!" Katherine shouted. She stepped around the fallen body of Dr. Akers and embraced Benjamin. "Benjamin, you're the best! What would I do without you?"

"Aw, you'd fare jus' fine, Miss Katherine."

Chief West and his deputy hurried over to Dr. Akers as he began to stir. Senator Bailey squeezed around them and stepped out into the sunshine. "Benjamin, how in tarnation did you know what was happening?"

"I was listenin' at the keyhole, peekin' ev'ry now n'again. When he pulled dat blade, I got plum riled up."

Katherine laughed and gave Benjamin another tight hug.

"Thank you, Benjamin," Senator Bailey said. "I was really worried this wasn't going to end well."

"It's not over yet." Agent Clay had joined them outside. "Senator, Chief West and his deputy are taking Dr. Akers to the county jail to hold him until I get there."

The senator nodded, "Sounds good."

Agent Clay turned toward the door of the morgue and shouted, "Agent Todd!"

Agent Todd stuck his head out the door, "Agent Clay, Neal is waking up."

"Okay, good. Todd, ride with these men to the jail." Turning to Chief West, he said, "I know you are very capable and don't need Agent Todd's help. But now that we have Dr. Akers in custody, we're not letting him out of our sight. When I'm through here, I'll join you at the station."

"Yes, sir!" replied Chief West. He hoisted up the dazed Dr. Akers and escorted him to the waiting police wagon.

Agent Clay watched in silence as the wagon door was locked, leaving Dr. Akers trapped in the dark solitude of the mobile cell. Once satisfied that Akers was securely confined, he turned back to Katherine and Senator Bailey. "Now, we have another issue yet to deal with. Let's check on our patient." He extended his arm to offer them the lead, then followed them back through the door and into the morgue.

Chapter 23: Interrogation

It took a few seconds for Katherine's eyes to adjust from the sunshine of the outdoors to the poor lighting in the examination room. No one spoke as they entered; the only sound was the echo of their footfalls on the hard floor. As her vision cleared, she saw Neal sitting up on the examination table, slumped over and groggy as if he had just waked up from a three-day slumber. The naval officers stood in front and to either side of him as if they feared he would try to run away.

Agent Clay walked around the table, then stepped between the naval officers and took Neal by the wrist. Checking his pulse, he asked, "Neal, can you hear me?"

Neal nodded his head.

"Good. I don't mean to rush you, but we still have a mystery to solve. Do you understand?"

Neal nodded again.

Agent Clay continued, "Can you speak to me? Don't just nod. Tell me. Are you awake enough to speak and think coherently?"

He nodded and said, "Yes. Yes, I believe I can. But I have

a terrible headache."

"That's the chloroform," Agent Clay replied. "It'll wear off. May take a while, but the headache will go away."

"Can't wait."

Katherine laughed. Neal immediately turned to see her standing behind him. He held his hand out to her. "Katherine. I'm glad you're here."

She moved forward and took his hand in hers. "I wouldn't be anywhere else."

"Neal," Agent Clay interrupted, "these two men are from the Navy, both masters at arms. They want to ask you some questions concerning your departure from the ship, as well as the murder of the petty officer on board. Do you think you're up to that? Do you need more time?"

"No, sir, I'm good. I knew this time was inevitable, so I'm ready."

"Well," Agent Clay chuckled, "if you can muster the word 'inevitable,' then I think you're right." He turned to the Navy officers. "Men, you can begin whenever you're ready."

One of the officers stepped forward. "Petty Officer Crowson, my name is M. A. A. Charles Talbot. This is my assistant, M. A. Curt Mallory, who will be taking official notes. Are you sure you're up to questioning at this time?"

"Yes, sir. I'll be fine."

Talbot turned to his assistant, "Note that question and response, Mallory."

"Got it," Mallory said.

Talbot continued. "For the record, state your rank, name, and vessel assignment."

"P. O.—I mean, Petty Officer Neal Crowson, U. S. S. Virginia."

"Thank you, Petty Officer Crowson. From this point forward, P. O. will be fine."

"Understood, sir."

"Now, P. O. Crowson. On or about Monday, April 13, 1908, just off the shore of Baja California south of Tijuana, Mexico, were you or were you not, involved in an incident where one of your fellow petty officers was struck and killed, and subsequently, you and three seamen evacuated ship?"

"Yes, I was."

"Did you know the P. O. who was killed?"

"I'm not sure, sir. The men were actively involved in a struggle, and all I could see clearly was the officer's uniform."

"I see." Talbot paused to let Mallory finish his notes. Continuing, he asked, "Did you recognize the three seamen involved in the incident?"

"Yes, I knew all of them. They weren't in my group, but we crossed paths often."

"What were their names?"

"Seaman Buck Alford and his apprentice, Robbie Young. The third was Seaman David Ames."

"What kind of men were they?"

"As I said, they weren't in my group, so I didn't spend

much time with them. Actually, I avoided them. They were—" he hesitated but reluctantly continued, "they were troublemakers. Everyone had issues with them. That's why I tried to steer clear of them. Fortunately, I was able to get off to a good start in the service, and I didn't want to mess that up. So, I intentionally steered clear of them."

Talbot nodded, then began to pace again. Mallory continued to scribble on his notepad. "So," Talbot continued, "you say they were troublemakers. Describe what you mean by that. What kind of trouble were they creating?"

Neal thought carefully. "Stealing. Fighting. Telling lies about seamen they didn't like and getting one man pitted against another." He paused again. "Bullying. Extorting money from weaker seamen...."

"They were never caught?"

"Well, yes, I was told they had. I heard they had been reprimanded several times. But it never took long before they were back to their old habits."

As M. A. Mallory jotted down notes, M. A. A. Talbot paced back and forth in the small area in the back of the morgue behind the examination table. Katherine still held Neal's hand, rubbing it gently during the pauses between questions. The senator and Agent Clay stood against the wall, watching the scene unfold as if it was a motion picture—except this picture included sound, smell, and the threat of serious consequences.

Talbot stopped pacing and turned to face Neal. "P. O. Crowson, tell me your version of the incident. Start at the beginning, how you happened upon the struggle, what took place, and what happened afterward."

"Yes, sir. I already told you some of it, but I'll try to give you all the information I can.

"We were somewhere along the coast of Baja California, not too far out of San Diego, when I heard a faint scuffling sound. It sounded like it was coming from somewhere behind the forward guns. So, I went to investigate. I hurried over to the seaward side gun turret and found three seamen scuffling with a petty officer."

Talbot held his hand up as a sign for Neal to stop talking, allowing Mallory to catch up on his notes. After a few seconds, the scribbling stopped. Talbot motioned for Neal to continue.

"As I said, I knew these guys. Everybody on board knew these guys because they were rough characters. Buck was the tallest. He considered himself a leader and tried to take charge of every team project he was assigned to, even if he was outranked. Robbie was Buck's sidekick. He was a bit simple, you know, mentally. But he thought Buck hung the moon and would do anything he told him to do. David was— well, he was quiet but smart, always ready to get any edge or use any opening to manipulate the person or situation for his own gain. The P. O. I couldn't identify, but I recognized the uniform."

Talbot interrupted. "Okay, good. You got all that, Mallory?"

"Give me one second, sir." In a few seconds, Mallory finished his notes. "Go ahead, sir."

"Now, P. O. Crowson, tell me how you got involved in the scuffle."

"Yes, sir. When I saw the fight, I ran over to try to stop it. But I had just started their way when I saw Buck hit the P. O.

in the head with a pipe. He dropped to the deck like a sack of rocks, a gash in his head and blood going everywhere. I tried to get to him, but the three of them turned on me. They beat me pretty good, then threw me in the drink."

Talbot began pacing again, allowing Mallory a few moments to finish scribbling his notes. "You may continue now, P. O. Crowson."

"Well, the water was colder than I expected and pretty much jolted me to my senses. When I came back to the top, I could hear the other guys splashing around in the water. I saw a life ring floating nearby, so I swam over and grabbed it and started making my way to the shore. I guess the guys threw them overboard just before the fight started. Anyway, I wanted to get away from them as fast as possible, so I tried to put distance between us as fast as I could."

"Why is that?"

"Because I was the only witness that could identify them. If we made it to shore together, they'd turn on me again. Probably take me out of the picture for good. Then they could blame it all on me and say I drowned before getting to shore. That's three against one. I'd have no chance. And if I was out of the picture, there'd be no one to prosecute and no way to prove anything against them. They'd get off free and clear."

M. A. A. Talbot stared at Neal for a moment as if debating the merit of Neal's account. Without flinching, he said, "Interesting story. Could be what really happened, could it not?"

Neal was incensed. He glared at Talbot. For a moment, the two men remained motionless, neither speaking, blinking, or backing down. Katherine feared one of them was about to snap. She squeezed Neal's hand to break the tension. It was a slight motion that went unnoticed by everyone in the room except Neal and Talbot.

Neal responded, "Could be. But it's not!"

Talbot's stare softened. He turned and again started to pace. "Please continue, P. O. Crowson. Did all of you make it to shore?"

Neal took a deep break to reset his patience. Everyone felt the tension begin to recede as he answered Talbot's question. "When I got to the shore, I was able to spot Buck and Robbie nearly a mile down the beach. They made it. It took me a while to find David. He was floating in the surf a couple of hundred yards off the beach. I guess it was his life ring I found."

"That's logical," Talbot said. "Did they see you?"

"I don't believe so. I spent the night hidden behind some driftwood in a ravine. The next morning their voices woke me up. They were searching for me, but I stayed put until they were out of sight down the beach. I escaped to a small Mexican homestead later that day. The *señora* who lived there gave me *tortillas* and water, boiled water. And a change of clothes."

"Nice of her," replied Talbot. He paced a bit more, thinking of his next question while allowing Mallory to catch up. "After you left the company of the old lady, where did you go next?"

"I traveled by foot and wagon up to Tijuana and on to San Diego. Then I bought passage on the California Southern and rode to Houston."

"And you've been here all that time?"

"Well…no. I took the Rabbit line from Houston to Gibsland, Louisiana. My parents live just a few miles south of there in the town of Bienville, so I walked the rest of the way." He paused for a moment. "It only took a few days for the sheriff to find out I was in town, so I came back to Houston. Didn't want to put my parents in an awkward position with the sheriff. They've been friends for years."

Talbot butted in, "Okay. And from there, you met with Katherine off and on, hid out in the storage building, started playing ball with the local team…and so forth."

"That's correct."

Talbot paused momentarily. "Okay, that's enough of all that," he said, shaking his hands in front of his chest in dismissal. He turned toward Neal and crossed his arms in front of his chest. "You claim that Seaman Buck Alford struck the P. O., correct?"

"Yes."

"What if I told you that both Alford and Young swore that it was you who murdered the P. O."

"As I said earlier, I suspected they would," Neal answered. "I wouldn't expect them to be honest. Would you?"

Clasping his hands behind his back, Talbot turned and took a couple of short steps away from Neal. For a moment, he stood in place, silent, moving one hand up to his chin as if in deep thought. The scratching of Mallory's pencil stopped. Pivoting suddenly, Talbot again paced and began to summarize.

"So, P. O. Crowson, let's get back to the critical information. For the record, restate the names of the men who were involved in the scuffle aboard the ship."

"There was Seaman Buck Alford, Seaman Apprentice Robbie Young, and Seaman David Ames. And the P. O., of course."

"And yourself."

"No, sir, I wasn't in the scuffle; I tried to stop it."

"Yes, right," Talbot replied. Mallory continued to scribble. "And who was it who struck and killed the P. O.?"

"It was Buck. Seaman Buck Alford."

"And you're sure of that?"

"Absolutely!"

Talbot turned to Mallory. "You have all of that?"

"Yes, sir," Mallory answered.

Talbot shifted his gaze to Agent Clay. "That's all we need, sir. I believe we're done here."

Agent Clay leaned over and shook Talbot's hand. "Thank you." Talbot and Mallory turned and began to walk toward the exit door.

"Wait a minute!" Neal said, staring at M. A. A. Talbot. "Is that it? You're done?"

"Yes, we are," Talbot answered.

"Well...well, where does that leave me?"

"Petty Officer Crowson, when I questioned Seaman Buck Alford and Apprentice Robbie Young, I could tell who was the leader and who was the follower. I could also tell that Apprentice Young was a bit—simple, to use your words. So,

I questioned Alford first. He blamed you, of course. Then I questioned Young. He also blamed you. So, banking on the lower mental sharpness of Apprentice Young, I told him that Seaman Alford blamed the killing on him. I said, 'Young, Seaman Alford said you hit the officer in the head with a steel bar.' Ha! That scared him to death. He screamed, 'No! Buck did it! Buck hit him with a pipe!' Then he spilled the beans. Told the whole story, which, by the way, exactly matched yours. Including the part where they threw you overboard. So, all I needed was your version of the incident to corroborate Young's."

Neal stared in disbelief. "You mean I'm free?" He glanced at Katherine then back to M. A. A. Talbot.

Talbot smiled. "Yes, sir. Completely vindicated. You are free to go."

Neal spun around and jumped off the examination table into Katherine's awaiting arms. He threw his arms around her and lifted her off the floor, dancing around the room in complete jubilation. Senator Bailey joined them, rejoicing in the confirmation of Neal's honesty and integrity and in the emotional triumph of legal vindication.

As they stepped out the door of the dark morgue, they were met by Benjamin's bright smile. "I heard it all, Miss Katherine! I's out here jus' celebratin' wit' you and Mr. Neal!"

Katherine replied, "You should've come in and celebrated with us, Benjamin!"

"No, ma'am! I ain't goin' in dat room 'til my las' day! An' I'm prayin' dat's a *long* time acomin'!"

Everyone laughed with Benjamin.

As the last of the group stepped into the sunlight, Veldon Maxwell approached Neal. He extended his hand for a shake. "Congratulations, young man!"

"Thank you, Mr. Maxwell."

"I followed the authorities over. There was no way I could go home without getting the end of the story."

Neal laughed. "And thank you for being part of the story. Only God knows what would've happened if you hadn't delivered that note."

"And speaking of that note," Neal said as he turned and placed his arms around Katherine's waist, pulling her close. "When did you come up with this plan for me to 'die' at the game? That's pretty morbid, young lady! Makes me wonder about you." He grinned.

Katherine laughed. "Oh, just a stroke of genius. I'm known for that, you know. A little genius here, a little genius there—"

"Oh, is that what it is?"

"Of course!"

"Of course. And was Agent Clay in on it?"

"Yes. He wasn't sold on the idea at first, but he came around."

"Why didn't you tell me? Would've been nice to know ahead of time."

"Agent Clay asked me not to tell you. He said it was important that you just focus on the game." Katherine chuckled. "I think he thought you'd panic and run."

"Panic and run! What? Where is that guy?"

As Neal turned to scan the group, Veldon Maxwell approached again. "Neal, I'm about to drive back to Shreveport. Is there anything you need? Can I contact your parents about your vindication?"

"Thank you, Mr. Maxwell. I'll send them a wire today." Neal had a sudden thought. "Wait! That brings up a good question." He searched the group, spying Agent Clay talking to M. A. A. Talbot. "Agent Clay!"

Clay turned around to see who had called. Neal, with Katherine in tow, approached him. "Agent Clay, Mr. Maxwell has offered to tell my parents that I've been cleared of all charges. But how will the sheriff know?"

Clay turned to M. A. A. Talbot, who quickly answered. "I'll be calling the Department of the Navy today to clarify your status. Washington will immediately send a bulletin to law enforcement agencies across the country. Your sheriff will be notified in a day, two at most. Don't worry; he'll find out long before he discovers you're back home."

"Thank you." Neal smiled and put his arm around Katherine.

"P. O. Crowson," M. A. A. Talbot called. Neal turned to meet his gaze. "The Navy thanks you for your service and would welcome you back should you so desire. With a promotion, of course."

"And don't forget the Shreveport Pirates!" Mr. Maxwell shouted. "We still want you, too!"

Everyone laughed. Neal replied, "Thank you, sirs, both of you. However, at the moment, I think my desire is focused on another subject."

Katherine swatted him on the shoulder. "You're such a cad!" They all had another laugh.

"Okay," Talbot said, "take your time. But do give it some serious thought. We'd be glad to have you back."

Neal nodded. "I will." Then, he, Katherine, and Senator Bailey made their way to the car where Benjamin was waiting, with all the car doors open.

"I don' know who's sittin' where, but de' do' is open."

Katherine laughed. "Neal and I will sit in the back. You don't mind, do you, Father?"

Senator Bailey chuckled. "Under the circumstances, I believe that would be fitting."

"Well, all aboard then!" Benjamin said. He waited as Katherine and Neal got comfortable on the rear seat, then closed the door behind them. By this time, the senator had closed his own door. Benjamin trotted to the front of the car, turned the crank handle to start the engine, then climbed behind the steering wheel. "Any place special you all wanna go?"

"Home, Benjamin," the senator said. "Just take us home."

The words gave Katherine contentment, peace. She was sincerely happy for the first time in months, maybe for the first time ever. All was well in her world. Despite the heat of the day, she pressed herself boldly against Neal and held him tightly, as if he would try to get away.

Neal made no objection. Rescued from the stress, anxiety, and despair of what had seemed a hopeless situation, he savored every moment of this unfamiliar but welcomed tranquility and the unique emotional completion a man gets from a loving woman. There were things yet to do; he knew that. But those things were good and would come to fruition naturally, sequenced and completed as time requires.

Chapter 24: The Cruise

"I've got it!" Katherine shouted. "It's the most wonderful idea!"

"I can't wait to hear," Neal smirked.

"We could take the train to New York, stay there for a few days, then board the Lusitania and take a cruise to Liverpool! Wouldn't that be amazing!?"

"I know what you're trying to do, Katherine. You want to get me back on the ocean to find out whether or not I miss the sea. I know what you're up to."

"It's not about that, Neal! It's about our honeymoon." She sat down beside him on the couch. "I want it to be the best ever, something we'll never forget. Something we can tell our children and grandchildren about." She took his hand in hers and added, "Something romantic."

Neal squeezed her hand and smiled.

Katherine continued, "You need to get away for a while and clear your head. Then you can be more objective about accepting Father's job offer. And," she paused, "you need to make sure you'll be content on dry land."

"I knew it! I knew that was what you were up to!"

Katherine stood and turned her back to Neal. "Well, you do need to make sure. And I want a romantic honeymoon. Is that too much to ask?"

Neal stood up behind her. "Look. A train ride from Houston to Beaumont would be romantic as long as I'm with you."

"Oh, shush! You know you want a good, long honeymoon as much as I do."

"That's what I want, yes. But what I need is to decide on my future, our future. The Navy is out, I promise you. I need to decide whether to stay here and work in the oil business for your father or go back to Louisiana and pursue civil engineering with Dad and Albert. Or baseball."

Katherine turned to Neal and placed her arms on his shoulders, cupping her hands behind his neck. "You can do that on the cruise. Father told us there is no rush for your decision; we can take as much time as we need. The cruise will clear our minds and give us a new perspective. Please, Neal, do it for me, for *us*."

Neal looked deep into her pleading eyes, admiring the beauty, honesty, and openness staring back at him. "You know, you don't make it easy for me to be obstinate."

Katherine laughed. "Good." She pressed her lips to his in a short, light kiss. "We'll have plenty of time to plan our future on the ship."

Neal laughed. "Okay, I suppose it couldn't hurt. Besides, the White Star Line in Liverpool is designing a much bigger luxury ship that's supposed to be the most lavish ship on the seas. I'd love to do a little research on it while we're there."

"That's interesting," Katherine replied. "Have they named it yet?"

"I'm not sure." Neal paused. "You know, maybe we should postpone our cruise until that one is commissioned."

"Not a chance!" she said, swatting him on the shoulder.

"They claim it'll be the biggest cruise ship in the world and the safest. Unsinkable, they say."

"Who says?"

"You know...*they* do."

"Uh-huh," she said as she turned away. "We're not putting off our honeymoon!"

"Come on, Katherine," Neal teased. "It'll only be a year or two."

She pivoted around to face him. "You're always playing games!"

"I distinctly remember you telling me to do just that."

"Uh, that was 'once upon a time.' I didn't mean ever after. It doesn't make me happy!"

"I'm sorry, you're right," he said. "But it would be interesting to review the cruise schedule for that ship. It may be going to some very exotic locales."

"Maybe," she admitted. "But, by the end of our honeymoon cruise, I'll have a better idea of what kind of husband you're going to be."

"What does that mean?"

"Well, if you're a good husband, I might consider the other cruise."

Neal smiled, "And if not?"

"If not," Katherine grinned, "then before the first cruise is over, I'll hire a couple of reprobates to throw you overboard."

"Oh, no, ma'am! My ocean swimming days are over!"

Katherine laughed. "Well, remember this, mister, I'm a woman of my word. Just ask Father."

"Nope, don't have to." Neal smiled, "I believe you."

"Good," Katherine replied with a sly grin. Placing her arms around his waist, she pulled him close and rested her head on his chest.

Neal relished her frequent acts of affection and was glad to reciprocate. He wrapped his arms around her, closed his eyes, and rested his chin on her head. He could feel every beat of her heart and relished the rise and fall of her chest with each breath. No one ever made him feel this way before. In these precious seconds of intimacy, Neal felt total comfort, security, and peace.

After a moment, she gazed up into his eyes and whispered, "I want our journey to last a lifetime."

Neal smiled. "If I have anything to say about it," he replied, "it will last for eternity."

The End

Afterword

Uncle Neal kept a personal journal while a sailor on the U. S. S. Virginia, one of the ships in President Theodore Roosevelt's Great White Fleet. After his untimely departure from the ship, the Navy returned this handwritten journal to Neal's family, and it ended up in the hands of Neal's closest brother, Albert, my grandfather. It was later inherited by my father, who passed it down to me.

I had heard Neal's story at a very young age, but it was years later before I read his journal. His personal accounts were fascinating, filled with vivid descriptions of exotic locations and scattered with notes about travel, weather, and events on the seas. I was immediately drawn in, wanting to know all about him and wanting to know more about this voyage launched in the first decade of the twentieth century.

My research didn't reveal much about Neal, so I had to rely almost wholly on the family version of his life. But it unearthed more than I could imagine about the Fleet, the Jamestown Exposition, and events that occurred during both. Somewhere along the way, it occurred to me that this event has been literarily unexploited, unvoiced, unlike the Titanic or the Hindenburg or the romanticizing of the American West. I knew I had to write a book. But not just a factual account of the journal or the voyage; that would be boring. I had to write a novel, an adventure, a romance based on Neal's written words and the events of his life which occurred afterward. So, a fiction novel it would be.

Much of Neal's story portrayed in this book is true. Much of it is pure fiction. But he was, in fact, a farm boy, a sailor, a fugitive, a writer, and a baseball player. He did end up playing baseball for a team in Houston, and they did win the championship. However, his death wasn't faked. During the team celebration after the winning score, when everyone was cheering and throwing hats and gloves into the air, Neal was struck in the back of the head by a sailing catcher's mitt. Less than two weeks later, he succumbed to complications of a broken neck.

True Characters and Actual Events

This is a work of fiction inspired by the life and personal journal of Thomas Neal Crowson. True events and non-fictional characters are listed below. All other places, events, incidences, and characters in this book are either the product of the author's imagination or used in a fictitious manner. Any resemblance to actual persons, living or dead, or actual events is purely coincidental.

Non-fictional Characters

Thomas Neal Crowson—alias "James Landis."

Richard Crowson—Neal's father.

Fannie Crowson—Neal's mother.

J. E. Curry—Bienville Parish Sheriff.

Martin W. Littleton—Exposition Ball moderator, 1907.

Samuel Clemens (Mark Twain)—Introduced Rear Admiral P. F. Harrington, Exposition Ball Speaker.

Rear Admiral Purnell F. Harrington—retired U. S Navy.

Charles Evans Hughes—governor of New York.

Claude A. Swanson—governor of Virginia.

Grover Cleveland—past President of the United States.

Robert Fulton Ludlow—grandson of Robert Fulton.

Mrs. Donald McLean—President-General of the Daughters of the Fathers of the Republic.

Hunter Hill—coach of the Houston Buffalos baseball team.

Charlie Middleton—player for the Houston Buffalos.

Pat Newnam—player for the Houston Buffalos.

Actual Events

Jamestown Exposition of 1907.

Robert Fulton Day Ball.

Voyage of the Great White Fleet.

Equatorial initiation by 'Neptune Rex.'

Murder of the Petty Officer on the U. S. S. Virginia and subsequent desertion of the sailors.

Baseball game in Houston (actual team unverified).

About the Author

Joel Crowson was the sixth of seven children born to a career military father and a "domestic goddess" mom. Just before his seventh birthday, his father retired from the military and moved the family to a rural property near Hodge, Louisiana. Joel spent his spare time fishing, hunting, camping under the stars, collecting relics, playing guitar, and following his imagination, which earned him the nickname Dreamer. To date, Dreamer has three patents.

He began writing at an early age, receiving many compliments from his teachers, and winning a regional poetry contest in middle school. His technical manuals have been translated into twenty-five-plus languages and sent to countries all over the globe. As a freelance writer, he has written many poems and lyrics and has published many newspaper and magazine articles. His favorite literary genre is historical fiction. *Play the Game* is his first full-length novel.

Joel now lives with his one and only, Anna Beth, near Haughton, Louisiana.

CPSIA information can be obtained
at www.ICGtesting.com
Printed in the USA
LVHW050754130422
715961LV00008B/314

9 781685 563189